THE LIFE

A WORTHLESS ANALYSIS

DHIRANJAN PATRA

Made with ♥ on the Notion Press Platform
www.notionpress.com

Contents

Acknowledgements

The net abode of my divine mentor—the unseen power that governs the universe—spontaneously inspires me to recollect the criss-cross of memories, visions, observations, analyses, and introspections. This fosters a profound sense of creative ecstasy within me. I am deeply touched by the great thinkers and writers of my native state, especially the legendary Manoj Das and Fakir Mohan Senapati.

My innate instinct, responsiveness, and sensitivity compel me to voice the sorrows and sights surrounding countless destitute homes, striving to find a glimmer of hope even in the verdant gloom of rainy nights. I cherish the memories of my teachers, well-wishers, and friends who believed in me, guiding me through moments of confusion and riddles.

My unwavering temperament for reading and exploring diverse facts continually teaches me the value of remaining an ignorant learner until my final breath. I firmly believe that every individual is unique and purposefully designed to uncover the essence of life through introspection.

I seek to inspire readers to evoke their sensible reactions to the social anecdotes that surround us. Literary creativity, to me, is an emotional outburst—a form of pure madness yearning for an outlet. My inspiration stems from all the great thinkers, writers, and pioneers of modern India who have adorned the world with their noble contributions, offering us the opportunity to learn and grow.

Among freedom fighters, Netaji Subhas Chandra Bose holds a special place in my heart, as do modern leaders like

Atal Bihari Vajpayee and the tallest leader of Odisha, the son of Kalinga, Sri Biju Pattanaik. Their ideals fill me with an enduring hope for a world characterized by freedom, dignity, and democracy in every walk of life.

Prologue

As the calling bell rung he said;

Wait, I am going to open the door. You have arrived in time. It is going to be 8 P.M. Manas came out of his nostalgic mood. He had taken the pain of recollecting all unexpected turn of events in life. He couldn't keep his mind in leash when things started happening to him without planning. Perhaps puberty made him a fool. He got demented for love and sex. His guilty consciousness made him realise all undeserving and un avoidable cross currents of life are a part of universal enigma. He condemned himself for crusading his widow mother's dream and expectations. In a state of agog he felt all analysis of the be gone days worthless. Read the novel to know why life compels us to compromise with many things and kindles the unbeaten zest for living with hope for something better from dejavu of Manas Mazumdar.......

1

CHILDHOOD

CHAPTER 1

Mr Manas Mazumdar of Malatipur had taken two days CL from office as his wife and children had gone to Lord Shiva Chandaneswar Temple to attend marriage party of their kindred Birendra Giri. Manas had to look after his house and take care of the pet dog named Bazigar. It was 2 PM in the month of January. He had taken meal from local Rameshwar Continental Hotel at Bada Bazar of Malatipur town. The pet dog ate mutton curry and rice and he himself took vegetarian meal as it was Tuesday. He had the conviction that without piousness and divine pursuits, human become distinctly animal in thoughts and sensibilities. That is why as per his routine life, he takes non-veg meals only on Wednesday and Friday.

His pet dog was sleeping under his cot and snoring like an innocent but very active and sensitive child. While laying in his cot his eyes fell on image of his demised mother kept on the shelf. It took him back to all begun days of his childhood, accidental death of his father, helplessness of his widow mother, his school days, college days, his youth, love affair, marriage, fatherhood and struggling present. The life that he has started with zero or perhaps with some dots moved on a curvy path surrounded by many incidents that became his best school of life. He felt the necessity to record his thoughts with flash backs as it was appearing life weaves on the surface of the water.

He closed his eyes, slept in bed and preferred to rotate the coils of cinematography episodes appearing like weaves on the surface of water in his sub-conscious mind. First of all, the most sensational and griping image of a corner of their corn field with little water and wild fishes became very glaring and alluring. It was 31 October one or two days before Deewali, his widow mother got up from bed at 6 AM, finished his all household routine work and got ready to go for fishing carrying a small tin bucket and silver plate. In those days the prices of vegetables was very high. Being an impoverished state, she had left the common cult of eating vegetarian meals in the holy month of Kartik. She was aware that fish curry would be affordable for five members of her family including her mother-in-law and three children. Manas was reading in Class III, a boy of 8-9 years of age, he was much attached to his mother. He could not miss his mother's present as he found parental care in her. His mother was the whole world, the life and all teachings for him.

That was a big corn field of 3 acres periphery. Tall paddy corps were standing with pollination and waiting for ripening. Her mother showed him the golden paddy corps and said ; when I entered into my father-in-laws house at the age of 18, my father-in-law was the then Headmaster of our village School. Our family had the blessing of Goddess Laxmi and Sarswati. The death of my father-in-law after

15 years snatched all glory by and by and the next episode came in shape of death of your father. Your elder brother was only 10 years when I took the whole burden of family and the risk of total cultivation of the land in my own hand. From those days till today, I feel joy of visiting the corns fields every morning and in the afternoon, it is became a part of my inner joy like that of visiting any function. Manas listen to his mother and thought why his mother was whiling away time telling her all these things which he could not understand at his age. In the later years, after death of his mother he realised the importance of her words as a part of motivation how to shoulder responsibility.

Mother and son got busy with catching fishes from the ditch at the corner of the paddy field. It was an interesting hide and seeks play of the wild fishes under the faggots. She folded her white sarees as a lungi and went on pressing the mud after draining water of the ditch with tin bucket. Manas was standing and watching his mother's mastery in catching fishes. It took almost two hours of exercise in draining water, catching fishes and carrying them back home. Now Manas got ready to test fish curry with saliva on his tongue. His mother could not help laughing and said :-

"Why you are so impatient. We are not going to eat raw fish or nobody is stealing the fish. Let me finish the pre requisite process of washing the fish and making it ready for fry. Manas became very happy and said Mother, I pray God, every day you catch fish and let us it palatable meal. Mother said nothing but smiled."

In those days, Manas looked upon his mother, an open book of duty and responsibility. Sometimes she seemed to him a complex encyclopaedia. How she originate such prudent thoughts, how she respond to the situations so quickly and why she never get tried up doing this and that from morning to late night. How she never feel afraid of anything or anybody. In the middle of night how she dared to move around the house carrying a kerosene Lantern. Their house was at the corner of the village. It was almost a lonely house apart from instant neighbours. These are the questions that very often confused him. He remembered another incident when he came ray away to communicate the news that he had heard sound of clustered fishes at the corner of another paddy field, but mother smiled and said, things are not what they sound and seem. The small fishes are very few in number make a great noise in scanty water. You should not go for making your body anointed with mud for catching a few minnows. In the likely way, his elder brother sometimes made wrong estimations of telling that the harvest from paddy would be 60 quintals, mother was very quick and accurate to show the calculation of total paddy harvest from his parental tillage of 5 acres and 70 decimals.

Whie Manas was bringing the glimpses from unconscious to subconscious and to record in black and white as a conscious adult mind he felt the cut and decided to wait for the next flow for recording what the life says.

CHAPTER 2

On the next day that was 2nd December , a chilly morning, his maternal grandmother arrived at his house at 6.30 in the morning and shouted ;

Basundhara, I have arranged oxen to carry paddy bundles from the field. They are coming with oxen to bring paddy bundles from field to home. Manas's mother Basundhara said;

Let them come after one hour. Half of the cut paddy plants are not yet tied up to bundles for shifting to the backs of oxen. In the mean while I am going to tie up the hay of cut paddy plants into bundles. I have also hired a wager to cut paddy plants . He will assist me. So that there will be no problem to shift the paddy bundles from field to home.

Mother got ready for her journey to the field. She assigned the work of watching goats and cows to Manas and took her two sons to assist her in binding paddy bundles. Manas gave straw and husks to the cows and calves and grass to the goats. The maternal grandfather also went to the field carrying rope and sickles in his hand. It was Sunday. So Manas also took the responsibility of carrying parched rice, green chilly, onion and pickle to the field for everybody working there. His mother had made all arrangements of tiffin before leaving home for fields.

Manas arrived at their corn field carrying tiffin at 10 A.M. He found his mother crying and holding her injured thump and fore finger already bandaged with cloth. The bandaged cloth was wet with bloods. Keeping all tiffin items and water pot he ran to home to bring mustard oil. He ran to home as first as he could and again ran to the field carrying mustard oil bottle and a clean torn napkin cloth.

Maternal grand father removed that blood soaked cloth from injured fingers , poured mustard oil on injuries and again bandaged with the clean napkin cloth. Manas looked at her mother's face with wistful eyes and started sobbing. His mother wiped out tears from his eyes and said;

Why are you crying? While cutting paddy the sickle touched thumb and fore finger of my left hand. The pain is going to stop after a few minutes. You go back to home. Keep watch on domestic animals and prepare your lessons. Manas said;

Let me stay here and assist you in cutting paddy. You take rest. Eat tiffin, drink water and instruct us to do the needful.

Mother smiled. She knew that Manas wouldn't leave her. She said to her eldest son Mahesh and middle son Soumesh to serve tiffin to everybody . she didn't eat. Manas and his two brothers compelled her to eat. Mother and sons ate together.

Having eaten tiffin she wanted to cut paddy plants with sickle. Her father said;

Don't take risk. Again bleeding might take place. Iam going to Natasir's shop to buy some tablets for relieving pain and repaining injuries.

Manas and his brothers helped the wagers to load paddy bundles and the oxen started carrying paddy to home. It continued for thee hours. At 1 P.M all of them returned home for lunch and rest.

Grandmother had cooked hot rice and egg curry. All of us dined together. Mother remained at home. Our grand mother, maternal grand father and wagers went to the field and completed the task of bringing paddy bundles to home in the evening.

CHAPTER 3

In the evening mother, grandmother, maternal grand mother and maternal grand father sat on the verandah and discussed about their experience of the super cyclone which had taken place in the year 1971. Manas and his two brother listened to the tales of the past about a natural calamity. Grand mother was a good story teller.She narrated the story with pathos, suspense , humour and adventurous fortitude of the Cyclone victims.

On the day of super cyclone falling on the land the wind blew above 180 kilometre per hour. It uprooted many trees, broke thousands of houses, destroyed paddy fields and flooded the whole locality. It snatched lives of thousands of animals, birds and men, women and children. Manas wanted to know what had happened to their house. Mother said;

Our two storied mud house with thatched roof gave shelter to almost 20 families of our village whose walls crumbled and thatched roof was blown away. Manas said;

How you saved our house?

Mother said;

We tied strong jute ropes to the main bamboo used in the thatched roof and tied other end of the rope to the deep rooted bamboo stray on the ground. We used more 100 hundred such strays to protect the thatched roof from high speed wind. The mud wall of our house is wide and strong enough to protect cyclone. So the villagers preferred to take shelter in our house. We kept all doors and windows of our house closed for the whole night and spent

sleepless night offering prayer to God. All our domestic animals also shared rooms with us. The families who took shelter had brought essential provisions like rice, potato, dal, parched rice, flattened rice, match boxex, lantern, torch, biscuits, onion, garlic, ginger, mustard oil etc.

Manas interrupted and said;

What had happened to all trees of our homestead land?

Mother said;

We had taken all precautions. All big trees at our homestead land had been branched off. We had all provisions for cooking food for more than hundreds of people.

Mahesh wanted to know about sufferings of the cyclone victims. Mother said;

Hundreds of trees were uprooted, near about80 percent of the houses of the village were destroyed. Walls crumbled, roofs blown away and small tress stood bald without branch and leaf. The carcases of birds, pariah dogs, stranded cattle were scattered here and there. The whole village looked like a grave yard. Crops and vegetables in the field were half destroyed due to two days of incessant rain fall and cyclonic wind.

After cyclone the people faced severe scarcity of food. The poor and the lower middle class were the worst victims. Some of them left village and went to kolkotta, surat and Hydrabad in search of job. Many old and handicapped died of cholera. People ate leaves of jute plant , tamarind tree and arum . The village became deserted.

Manas asked;

What steps were taken by Govt. for relief and rehabilitation?

Mother replied;

In those days poverty, illiteracy, disease, epidemic, starvation, drought, famine and flood were very common enemies of the people. Lack of communication and health care facilities were affecting the people. All over the cyclone affected districts thousands lost their lives. No safe is safe for the mighty nature. It is the ultimate creative and destructive mystery of nature. Cyclone and incessant rain fall created challenge for the Govt. and voluntary organisations to carry on rescue and relief work. There was hardly any road connectivity among the villages except muddy narrow roads full of ditches. That is why lakhs of people lost their lives. Aftermath of cyclone and flood was more challengeable. Cholera broke out. People died like insects and flies. It was not possible to cremate all dead bodies.

Again Manas asked;

Tell us about your own experience of the dreadful nights during cyclone.

Mother said;

I spent two sleepless nights chanting names of God and offering prayers to protect our lives. I had strong faith on His mercy. I believe that His will is the final truth. If He protects no frost can kill. So I told everybody to have patience and faith. I was confident of facing the calamity with precaution, courage, cooperation and surrender to divine will.

CHAPTER 4

It was 16th August, Thursday. Manas got ready by 8.30 A.M to go to M.E. School hostel with his books, dresses, utensils, bedding, soap, oil, tooth brush, tongue cleaner and other study materials packed in a tin box. The headmaster had advised him to stay in the hostel for devoting more time on study. His competitor a girl was staying in the hostel . He was first in his class and that girl was second. All teachers were confident that he would be topper in the district in N.R.T.S examination. Agarwal M.E. school is one of the oldest M. E. School of his area. Many students of Malatipur and its adjoining locality were reading in that school and staying in the hostel. The watchman-cum peon of the school Daitari Raj was an industrial man. He was managing marketing and cooking of the hostel. The headmaster and his family were staying in a small building attached to the school. His two daughters and a son were living with them. Every one of them loved Manas for his talent. He always occupied first position in the class and in all extra curricular activities like debate, essay writing and poetry recitation.

It was very painful moment for Manas as he was going to part from his mother for the first time in his life. His eyes were getting weight with tears. He had also seen tears in his mother's eyes. She was busy with cooking hot rice and fish curry. His family had two ponds full of fishes. She used to keep fishes like sheat fish, big gudgeon, scorpion fish and climbing fish in a big earthen pot with water and make fish curry. His mother, brother and maternal gand father were cating fish with trammel and with fishing rod. So there was plenty of fishes in stock for curry. Manas used to enjoy fish curry in his house for five days in a week except Monday and Thursday.

When Manas was eating hot rice and fish curry a shower of heavy rain fall began and continued. Manas had to reach the school hostel before 10 A.M. As rain abated his middle brother carried his luggage and a wooden stand with shelfs for keeping books to the hostel. A big tin box packed with luggage and wooden stand was very heavy to carry but he carried it on the muddy road with much difficulty. The school was about 3 kilometre away from his house. Two brothers arrived at the school at 9.45 A.M. Leaving him at school hostel his brother returned back. He kept luggage in the hall meant for boarders and went to the class room.

After school hour he unpacked his luggage and put them in proper order by the side of his bed. Stewing mat on the ground he kept the tin box near his head adjacent to the pillow. As the sun set and evening put veil of darkness glistening with twinkling stars he felt inner urge to cry. The memories of his mother made him bewail. The picture of his mother burning incense sticks inside at basil plant citadel became alive in his mind. He used to sit beside his mother at God's room in his house. The watchman Daitari looked at Manas's eyes bulged with tears and called him to join in the prayer class. Though he attended prayer class his mind was not at all parting from memories of his house. His eyes streamed with tears and for the first time he felt himself very lonely like an urchin. Staying away from his mother and home was a very painful for him.He started sobbing and the headmaster's daughters came to console him. The headmaster's wife tried to console him with her affectionate words. She said to him;

You think that it is your home. I am your mother. You have two sisters and one younger brother. My two daughters Rajanigandha , Raktajaba and son Prakash are very happy to include you in our family. I feel that I have two sons and two daughters. Looking around the head master's house he saw one daughter listening to radio, the other one was setting fire to the hearth and prakash was reading his lessons. He wiped out his tears in a napkin put round his neck and returned to his room.

He opened English book and stated reading difficult words but the memories of his mother made him thoughtful. He felt unhappy as he couldn't help his mother at the need. Very often he served his mother when she cut her fingers while mowing grass or while tumbling with log with heavy load of paddy on her head. As the youngest son he was the only instant companion of her mother .His concern was his mother's well being. His elder brother and middle brother were not so caring for mother as they had been allotted their duties by mother. Middle brother had to look after cattle and goats. He had additional duty of purchasing grocery from the village grocer's store. His elder brother had footpath stall near the primary school gate. He was dealing with dry snacks like papad, parched gram, mixture, biscuit , chocolate, parched flattened rice and parched rice. Their village market was adjacent to primary school. So his elder brother had business even after the school hour.

He tried his best to push away homesickness from mind but failed. The ambiance of his home flashed up again and again. When he concentrated on reading odia literature all familiar images of his mother's routine works like digging soil, sowing seeds, levelling the furrows, sprinkling insecticide with broom, planting paddy plants, cutting and reaping crop crowded his mind. He closed odia book and again opened English book . He went on reciting lines from the poem Paper Boat. It relaxed him for sometime but a strong sense of loss and unhappiness clasped his mind.

Super for the boarders of hostel was served at 9P.M . All boarders had to stand in queue to receive meal and curry in their plates and basins. His serial was after 16 students. He had no patience to wait as it was a new experience for him. So he returned back to room without taking meal. The other students reported the matter to Daitari. After serving meal to the students in queue he called for Manas and gave him rice and curry. Keeping meal near his head he went to fetch a jug of water from school tube well. Returning to room he again came out to take salt, green chilli or onion from hostel kitchen. He a half rotten green chilli. When he started eating watery dal and fried ladies finger he couldn't control tears rolling down from his cheeks. He ate half of his meal and threw the rest in the dustbin kept near the tube well.

The headmaster had two milky cows. He fed the cows with thrown away rice of the boarders. He hardly gave attention on quality of food for the hostel boarders. Manas realised everything in the very first day of his hostel life. He started reading his lessons as it was his habit to study up to mid night. He couldn't know when slumber chained him. His sleep was racked with night mares. In dream he saw his mother crying. She burnt her hand while draining hot water from boiled rice pot. He got up from bed and came to the verandah. He saw a mother dog and her poppies snoring at ther corner of hostel verandah.

On the next day he wrote an application to the headmaster cum hostel superintendent to permit him for visiting his house, He complained of head ache, cold and severe mental agony of detachment from family. The headmastertook the application and said ;

Manas, your mother loves you very much. You are missing him. You can go to your home . your longing for home and mother can be solved if you will spend a few days in hostel. Manas nodded his head and came to his room to depart for his home.

He arrived at his home at 4.30 P.M. His mother was feeding cattle and his maternal grand father was catching fish in the pond with dragging net. He said,

Mother staying in the hostel cann't help me for better preparation of study. It is only waste of time for standing in queue for meals, washing dish and basin , sweeping room and doing all activities like bringing drinking water, washing clothes and many more. So Iam going to leave hostel.

Mother said;

I knew all. You decided to live in the hostel and I made all arrangements. You stay at home and read as usual.

Manas thanked his mother. He was really lucky to get a real mentor in his mother. He thanked God and went into his room to change dress.

CHAPTER 5

Another very memorable weird experience of his childhood was his anxiety for N.R.T.S .He had appeared in the N.R.T.S examination after passing M.E. School board examination in O grade but was not sure about his performance. On the day of examination he suffered from fever but attended the examination. He answered all multiple choice questions while offering silent prayer to Goddess Saraswati. His body was shivering and head was reeling. Within duration of the examination he vomited three to four times through the window. In a state of nausea he answered all questions with a strong sense of surrender to the will and mercy of his divine mentor Goddess Minerva.

Everyday he offered prayer to Goddess Saraswati to make him successful in N.R.T.S. examination. Finally that joyous moment of divine grace came to him like a shower of rain at noon of a scorching heat summer season.The peon of M.E. School came to his home and communicated the news that Manas had stood first in his block to avail of N.R.T.S. The head master and his family members wanted him to meet them.

Manas's mother served parched rice, mixture, coconut slice, onion and green chilly to the peon. He relished everything and accompanied Manas to the school hostel. It was going to be 4.30P.M. when he arrived at school the headmaster came running to him and hugged him. His daughters and wife burst into tears because of over joy.The headmaster's wife poured all her affection on him. They looked upon him like a jewel and glory of the school. The peon Giridhari distributed sweets among the students. They treated Manas like a celebrity.

Manas returned from school in the evening. He saw his mother offering evening lamps to God. She was standing in front of the photographs of Goddess Saraswati, Laxmi, Durga , Radha and Krishna. She was deeply engrossed in devotion and gratitude to God and Goddess. Tears of joy was rolling from her cheeks.Her son's success was her happiness. She had a big dream in her son's career. She believed that her son Manas would bring glory not only for the family but for the whole locality.After evening prayer she opened her eyes and said to Manas;

I have offered you to Her divine grace. Mother Goddess Saraswati is your guardian angel. She will fulfill dreams of a poor mother like me. I surrender to her kindness. Manas bowed down before his divine mentor.

His maternal uncle and aunty arrived at Manas's house. He was headmaster of an M.E. school . He was teaching enghlish traslation to Manas when ever he got Govt. holidays. He was a manm of broad mind and heart. He was very glad at Manas's success and promised to gift him a new dress.

Manas's mother made delicious chicken curry and hot rice for night meal. All of them celebrated the evening foreseeing a golden future of Manas.

In the next morning his uncle and aunty went to market taking Manas and his middle brother with them. They purchased new paint and shirt for Manas and two paints for his middle brother and elder brother. They returned from market at 11A.M. Wearing new paint and shirt Manas started running on the village road. His village friends aswell as the elderly people greeted him for success and demanded sweets. Manas laughed as he knew that they wre making jokes.One of his friend shouted;

Manas, let us goto our village grocer's shop and share 1 rupees mixture together.Your mother will pay to him.

When the two friends arrived at village grocer's shop it was going to be half past eleven of summer days. Many villagers were sitting under the banyan tree adjacent to the shop. All of them praised Manas and hoped for his

Health , happiness and more success.

His uncle and aunty got ready for their return journey. They embraced him and said;

God has gifted you with exceptional talent. We pray the all mighty to shower more success anf glory on you. May God guide you at every step of your career.Manas touched their feet and they embraced him . Manas's mother raised her hands upward as a sign of her surrender to His will. Her elder brother blessed her and went to his home.

CHAPTER 6

Manas took admission in Balasore zilla school. He lived in the hostel to get his scholarship money from Govt. His first day experience was not pleasant. He felt himself very lonely and alienated from his sweet home. He stewed his bedding on the cot, put his box , plastic bucket, mug, dish, basin and glass under the cot. He put his books and notes on the small study table. He sat on the cot and started thinking about his mother and village .As the evening approached he felt inner urge to cry.

The sight of his mother burning evening lamps, his grandma setting fire to argols to drive away mosquitoes, their she goat giving milk to her kids, cows and oxen eating straws flashed up in his mind. Tears flooded his eyes. He was wiping out tears with his towel. His room mate , a boy of Basta named Girija came to console him. He narrated his painful experience of first day in the hostel. Manas listened to his story as he wanted to divert his mind from his sweet home and affectionate mother.

Girija had a group of friends in his village. They used to play Kabbadi in the afternoon till dusk. Sometimes they had competition in running from their village Shiva temple to the high school gate. They enjoyed the joy of swimming in the panchayat pond in front of Shiva temple. He felt very lonely and cried. He even left his meals and wanted to go home. His father came and took him to home. After two days he came to hostel taking one of his village friend with him. That friend stayed as a guest for two days and returned to village. Again he became unhappy . That unhappiness chased him for a week. There after he developed friendship with hostel guys and recovered from obsession.

He said;

It takes time to cope with any new environment. Strong mentality and friendship with others help to face new challenges. Every new comer to the hostel face the challenge to live alone away from home and village but after a few weeks all those obsession fade away. It happens as we part from family for the first time.

Manas smiled and said;

You seems right. Our mind is such. We have to control it. Attachment and detachment are the process. Let us go out of room and move in our school campus. The warden of the hostel was overhearing their conversation. He suddenly opened his mouth and said;

You are missing your home abode. You come to my residence at the back side of hostel.

Manas was reluctant to go there but the superintendent of the hostel came near them and said;

I have watched your disturbed mind because of your alienation from familiar environment. You visit our waden Bidura's house in every after noon and spend one hour with them before our evening prayer in the hostel. His wife is a high school teacher. She can help you in your study and give motherly care and affection.

Manas went to Bidura's house carrying English book and note book in his hand. When he arrived at the doorstep Bidura's wife Bandana came out smiling. She fondled him and took him to her bed room. Her daughter Kabita and son Minu accepted Manas as their elder brother. Bidura told his wife to give parched rice and mixture to all children. While eating they listened to songs in radio. While dressing vegetable with kitchen knife she said to Manas;

Always I collect information about the new comers to hostel. When you came to hostel he told me that you were a very good student and topper of your block in N. R. T.S. You have a bright future. You can enjoy study at different institutions when you will make friendship with strangers and turn the alien environment to homely environment. You take our home as your home and look upon me as your mother. The superintendent will never stop you visiting our home. You spend this evening playing with Kabita and Minu. I am going to make hot rice and delicious fish curry. We will eat together. He has taken permission of the superintendent.

She encouraged us to play poetry recitation competition. She also participated in it. Her voice was very soft and sweet. They enjoyed the joy of laughing and clapping . Kabita wanted to defeat Manas but Bandana helped him . So he became winner in poetry recitation. There after Bandana told them a story about her school days.

While living in High School hostel she had a room mate named Lilabati. Both were reading in class IX. Four girlswere living in a room. The other vtwo girls Rupali and Kalpana were reading in class VIII. Once both of them had gone to their homes. It was a rainy day. In the evening there was torrential rain and thunder.Bandana and Lilabati were hungry but they had no snacks. It was not possible to step out of room to purchase snacks. So they decided to break lock of kalpana's tin box that contained parched rice and mixture. They had seen when Kalpana put every thing in her box before leaving room. Parched rice, onions, dried chilly, mixture packet and pickle bam were inside her tin box.They broke the small lock hitting it with a small hammer. They pampered , parched rice, mixture, onion and dried leaves. It was raining like cats and dogs.

The weather was very congenial for crunching parched rice mixed with onion, dried chillies.

Kalpana arrived at the hostel on the next day. Finding her lock broken she asked Lilabati about it. She denied knowing anything of that matter. Bandana had gone for morning bath. Kalpana reported the matter to the superintendent of hostel Mrs. Suhagini Banerjee. She immediately called for Lilabati and Bandana to his office. Lilabati suggested her not to confess anything. Both of them arrived at the superintendent's office room. The superintendent asked her to tell the truth. She narrated the whole incident and begged forgiveness. The superintendent laughed and said;

You were hungry and it was raining. So you couldn't go outside to purchase anything from the shop infront of our hostel gate but it was your fault to break somebody's lock. You have to pay 25 rupees fine. Both of them agreed and returned to room.

The superintendent called for Kalpana to his room and gave 25 rupees to her for purchasing a new lock. Kalpana cried and said;

Madam, Bandana is like my elder sister. She loves me and guides me in study. So i willn't take money from my elder sisters.

The superintendent called for Lilabati to his office and said;

Why did you tell lies? You give an explanation about it.

She paused and asked kabita;

What lesson do you learn from my story?

She said;

We should speak truth. She again asked the same question to Manas and he said;

Truthfulness and candid confession of mistakes sweeten our relation and boost mutual trust, love and fellow feeling. Unnecessary lies must be avoided.

Bandana became very happy, SHE KISSED Manas's forehead and gave lord Jagannath's offal to him. She declared that she accepted Manas as her godson.

She told us to wash hands for eating supper. Her husband arrived at that moment. They enjoyed supper together sitting on the floor.

2

YOUTH

CHAPTER 1

Manas got higher first class in Matriculation examination and applied for admission in science stream in different colleges. As he had scored almost 80 percent marks in Matriculation he got intimation letter from all the colleges he had applied. He decided to study in Thomas Jefferson college at Udayapur. His college days made him more emotional and wild in temperament. The sight of beautiful damsels made him more crazy and sensitive. It seemed to him that company of beautiful damsels could bring all happiness to him. Every part of the beautiful girls and women seemed to him the greatest treasure on the earth. It became his routine work to gaze at beautiful girls. He minutely watched their feet, buttocks, nipples , pelvises, dimple cheeks, silky hair, rosy lips and shinning teeth. He spent hours together watching beautiful girls and women going on the road and thought about them. Very often he hovered in dream of getting married with a beautiful girl and enjoying sex with her. The film heroines appeared to his eyes the fairies on the earth. He purchased post card size photographs the then Hindi film heroines like Sridevi, Madhuri, Tabu , Rekha, Poonam and juhi and treasured their portraits inside books. While reading books his mind started dashing after them. Very often he gazed at their photographs and went for masturbation. While going to bed at night he imagined nude images of the beautiful women and spent many hours on sleepless pillow.

He watched every film and listened to romantic songs. His mind got engaged with sketching portraits women's private parts. The romantic scenes like a heroin drenching herself in rain, dangling her feet , lifting her saree above knee, bending down to show a part her breast and nipple, making braids of her silky hair, moving her hands on pelvis, winking and kissing the hero made him hyper sensitive. He became frantic to touch woman's private parts

His craze for sex with woman made him distracted from study. Hostel life seemed to him boring. He spent most of his time looking at girls and woman and thinking about beauty of their private parts of body. He neglected his study and managed to pass higher secondary examination in Gandhi division.

While regretting for such foolishness of youth he couldn't restrain one incident of his college days when he saw a very beautiful girl in red saree at a fair. Her turmeric anointed blonde body was glistening. Her wild eyes were inconstant like eyes of a doe. Manas came face to face with her when she was coming out of a temple at the north end of the fair closs the river Gobri. That was Radha Krishna temple.

There was a myth about that temple and fair ground. The king of that province had built the temple where his queen had lost one of her gold bracelet . Once the queen was roaming on horseback by side of river Gobri.The king looked up on her a deity. He built Radha Krishna temple to add religious austerity and cultural affinity of men with nature. The Makar fair of village Kajalpur had been celebrated from the year of establishment of the temple. It continued for seven days. The people of nearby town Malatipur and adjoining 10 to 12 panchayats visited the fair every year with their friends and relatives. The fair ground was full of mango groves. The natural abode of mango trees, river and temple on the bank of river made the fair ground more attractive.

The young men and women of the locality were very fond of visiting the fair. It gave them the opportunity to fall in love at first sight. Many couple confessed that they had seen each other at the fair and accordingly their marriage proposals were set and marriages took place.

His friend Harishankar's house was at kajalpur . He invited Manas to his home to see Makar fair. Two friends arrived at the fair ground in the afternoon. It was 3P.M. the fair ground was very crowded. His friend said to Manas;

You are looking like a film hero. Me seems you will hook your beloved from the fair ground. The rural damsels hardly miss the chance to leer at handsome young men of their choices. Many love affairs began in the fair had successful ending in happy marriage.

Manas smiled and said;

A good player always keeps his eyes fixed on goal post. I would be happy if i discover my dream darling at the fair ground. When they arrived at Radha Krishna temple Manas'seyes fell on a very beautiful damsel. She was coming out the temple. She looked like a fairy. Her gold ear rings, red colored saree with green border, green blouse, green nail lustre, green bangles, round fair face and rosy lips captivated him at first sight. Manas gazed at her and she smiled. He followed her from temple through out the fair ground. When she stopped near any stall to buy something Manas and Harishankar also stopped near that stall. She became sure that Manas had fallen in love with her. They spent all most an hour in the fair ground looking at each other and smiling but got no chance of talking. She was accompanied by her family members. After

one hour she came out of the fair ground and got into a trekker. As the trekker moved she smiled and waved her hand. Manas stood like a statue looking at her as far distance as his permitted.

Harishankar collected the fact that she was a girl of Malatipur town. The two friends returned to home in the evening. Manas became very unhappy. Harishankar said;

Let us forget her as dream. We may meet her at Malatipur town if luck permits us and if she is made for you.

CHAPTER 2

The gay nature and gross romantic sensibility made him victim to his imaginary mesh of searching for life in the company of dreamy damsel. His failure to maintain his standard in the examination shocked him but it was too late. He managed to pass his intermediate examination in science in Gandhi division. The new realisation of life made him look into life beyond such trivial and tangible pleasure of mere sensibility without sense. He repented for his abandonment of habits for mediation in every evening. It was his regular habits from childhood and he had adapted that habit when he was sitting with mother at God's room with folded hands offering prayer to show him the right way. His mother had taught him that there was nothing to beg from God as it is well known to the maker who is both in male and female form. A devotee has nothing to hide from him except a sense of atonement for misconduct and surrender to his mercy. He neglected two years thinking himself the maker of his destines and perhaps that was a pre destiny punishment for him to depart from the virtues way of life into dash after wayward wanton pleasure. He shared all his misconduct with one of his intimate friend who was an average student and had high esteem for inborn scholasticism.

He managed to part from that disillusion path of life and tried his best to concentrate all his energy for maintaining his standard as it was in matriculation in his B.A degree. The pace of life became more difficult for him as his mother and brothers also lost their faith as because they had extra ordinary anticipation from him. He could not make his heart transparent before his senior mentors but he had not lost his faith on himself. Instead of guilty consciousness he took bold decision to part from the bed habits one by one. In his intermediate degree he had gone far away in search of

entertainment. Visiting fairs, watching romantic feature films, Operas and listing to romantic songs had become his infatuation of unleashing lessons. As a first step he sold his pocket radio to one of his class mate and removed all photographs of film Heroes and heroines pasted on the wall of his hostel room. He kept distance from other friends who were regular visitors of film halls. Whenever a new film stared by Madhuri or Sridevi was released. A group of guys were almost frantic to enter into the film hall and took quaff all emotional jumps. After one year he found himself victim of another emotional pull though he had good bye to all these wayward habits that he had cultivated in his Intermediate years , but he could not avoid his love affair with a girl who came to his life in the first year of graduation. Knowingly or unknowingly or on a weak moment of puberty he fell in love with a girl at first sight. Actually, he visited that girl's family with one of his friend who brought his attention to the girl's affectionate mother who had lost one of his son and was living with four daughters. The lower middle class family was lamenting for the loss of their only son and was searching for any good guy who could assist the family with a blood relation bond. When he listen to the facts of that family and decided to visit them again perhaps it was his fault. In the later stage of life, when he analysed those days he could not agree as to why he was so emotionally inclined to the family. He had not taken the contract to compensate their loss or how he was sure that he was a good guy. Why he could not avoid that family? He was an emotional fool. He got caught in the reeve of love. Their second daughter who was reading in class nine was not so beautiful but had a big buttock and fleshy healthy body. Her two big nipples and buttocks attracted him and he couldn't control the temptation for sex. The girl's mother worked as a catalyst to tempt him. She deliberately embraced him and moved her hand on his thigh. When she found him getting hot she called her daughter and went into the kitchen and expected him to intercourse her daughter. One day she became successful.

Manas was caught red handed while enjoying their brunette girl. She took him to her chest, kissed him and said;

She is my daughter. How did you feel? Is she not sweet? Is it not the real joy of a young man? She laughed a coquettish laugh and moved her finger on his sense organ. She moved her tongue on her lips and said;

It is not so cool as I thought. Really you are my fit son-in-law.

Manas became very happy and kissed her. She went to her bed room laughing and rolled on a cot. At that time her daughters went out of house to play . Her husband had gone for shopping. She signalled him to come. As he came near her she held him tightly on her chest and said;

Manas you promise touching my head that you would marry my daughter Silpa. She would give you maximum pleasure . You promise.

Manas was about to say something but she hobbled her two legs around his waist and kissed him. He touched her head and said;

Yes,I promise to marry your daughter and get you as my loving sweet mother-in-law.

Her joy knew no bounds. She went on laughing and rolled on her cot . Manas was dump founded. Realising his nervousness she said;

My legs are aching. Press my legs and twist my toes.

She put her two legs on his lap and stated rubbing her heels on his thigh. He lifted her right leg to his chest and started licking her toes and heel.

She giggled and said;

How did you feel current of my body? I am 42 years old. Almost 20 years senior to you but you are caught in me. Aren't you?

Manas nodded his head. She fondled him and said;

Let me go out for pissing.

Manas said;

No, let me lick your two heels. She got up and patted him on back and said;

No, I can't control. I am going to give you the chance enjoying my daughter throught the night today. Be happy and smile. Let me go out for pissing.

Manas said;

Can I see you pissing?

She said;

No, I am your mother-in-law and trainer.

She caught hold of his sense organ and pulped that up and down twice and scrubbed her index finger on limy substance on his cloth. She laughed and said;

Are you happy or want my help more?

Manas said;

Yes , Iam happy.

She went out and returned after pissing . She sat beside him , tightly held his sense organ and said;

It is going to be evening. I have 20 minutes to be prepared for burning evening lamp. Let me make you more happy.

Manas said nothing. She repeated her drill with him and said ;

I am always ready to make you happy till your marriage.

Manas stayed in their house for that night. She told him not to bolt down door from inside. At mid night the mother and daughter tiptoed into his room and signalled him not to open mouth. Leaving her daughter inside she whispered to his ears;

Enjoy her for two hours. I will come to take her to our bed room at 3P.M.

He enjoyed shila but found her less hot than her mother. She came back at 3PM and signalled her daughter to go out. As shila went out she followed her to their room. She came back and slowly closed the door . She sat near his feet, stretched her two legs and placed on his chest. He got up and moved his hand on her thigh but she frowned and signalled him to sleep. As he slept she moved her heels on his sense organ and unbuttoned her blouse. She invited him to press her nipples.

His joy knew no bounds. He kneaded her two yellow colour nipples. She kissed him. In this way they spent the night till dawn.

In the next morning she requested Manas to spend another day with them and he agreed. Her husband went to his duty and all her daughters went to school. She took her bath near the tube well and asked Manas to come out of room. He loitered around her homestead land but kept his eyes on her blonde naked wet body. She was smiling while pouring water on her body and rubbing her fair parts. After bath she covered herself in towel and entered in to put on petticoat, blouse and saree. Manas came in and saw her putting on dress in front of him. He got tempted to touch her but she signalled him to go back.

Manas got angry with her and put on his paint and shirt. She came near him and said;

You can't control. Come and let me make you cool. She allowed him to embrace her from back and moved her hand rapidly on his sense organ. Within a minute he became cool. She collected the discharged limy substance in her palm and went to the tube well to wash her palm.

She came laughing and repeated the same drill. This time he felt tired . She said;

What is the matter? Is it not a pleasant game? Let me play the game till I feel urge for pissing.

Without waiting for any answer she kissed him and said;

Would you like to see me pissing?

He said;

Yes.

She laughed and said;

No, I will give you the chance to see only after you marry my daughter. You wait and have patience.

She went out to piss near a bush at her home stead land. Looking at Manas she signalled him to come and visit that spot where she had pissed. As manas went there she giggled and pressed his feet with her great toe and ran to her room.

Day to day Manas became frantic to marry shilpa. His mother-in-law always whispered at his ear to take licence. He forgot his family members and started living with shilpa's family. In one evening her husband and three un married daughters had gone to attend a function at nearby village. She called Manas to her room and closed the front door of the house. She told him to sit on her cot and stood before him biting her middle finger and leering at him. Manas pulled her to his lap. She crossed her hands around his neck , kissed him and said;

How did you feel? Is it not the greatest pleasure for you?

Before Manas could say something she pressed her buttock hard on his lap lifting her legs from the ground and said;

Held my two feet with your hands.

As he tried to do so, she lied on his chest and her dishevelled her hair on his face. He smelled scented oil of her hair and fondled her pinching her cheek. She changed her position and took him to her chest. While kissing him she said;

You marry my daughter as early as possible. You can play with her the whole night. Let me go to cook food.

She got up from bed pushing him to a side. She folded her saree,lifted it to a height and asked him to look.

As he looked she made her saree fall down and laughed a big laugh. She said,

Is it not the most beautiful thing for you?

Manas ran to her side, embraced from back and whispered to her ear;

Yes, very beautiful. Let me see it again.

She said;

No, you go to your home and tell them that you can't live without marrying Shilpa. I and my husband are going to give the proposal of marriage to your mother and elder brother. In your presence the matter will be resolved.

On the next day Manas went to his home but he couldn't disclose his love affair with shilpa. In the evening shilpa's mother and father visited Manas's house and gave the proposal of marriage. Manas's elder brother got angry at such a nonsense proposal. He said to Shilpa's mother;

You are a wench. You have pulled him to a sex trap. You have bewitched his young mind and heart. How do you dare to give such a shameless proposal? He is a scholar student. You want to kill his career and life.

Shilpa's mother Shrimantini roared like a lioness and said;

Your brother has defiled chastity of my daughter. She is carrying his child in her stomach. What can I do?

Manas's elder brother said;

Both you and your daughter are slatterns. It is your business. You go out of our home. Catch train and return to your home.

Shilpa's mother cried , looked at Manas and went out of the house. Her husband abused her.They went to the railway station which was 2 kilometre away from Manas's house .

In the evening Manas's mother said to Manas;

Don't betray that girl. You are guilty. I can't stop your brother as you broke his dream. You decide what to do?

She went to God's room and offered her prayer for half an hour. It was her routine work. Manas went to his room. He slept and went on thinking about Shilpa's mother Shrimantini. He felt as if she was whispering to his ears while lifting her saree and showing him her that beautiful yellow, black and red coloured spot within her thigh. He couldn't forget her. Her smiling face, her laughs, her dishevelled hair, her round buttock and her pelvis flashed up in his eyes. He decided to marry Shilpa and to make his mother-in –law happy. He spent the whole night only dreaming his mother-in-law.

In the next morning his elder brother said to his mother;

I have decided to held Manas's marriage in the next month. He must go to inspect a bride who is working as a nurse in a govt. dispensary. The negotiator Birendra is coming to accompany him to Nampo Bazar for bridal inspection. She is hundred times smart,educated, beautiful and superior to that characterless girl and her mother. This girl is a very attractive blonde. Her father is a high school head master. They are agree to the proposal as Birendra had told every thing to them.

I can't tolerate that a post graduate student in English will marry a fat matriculate brunette of a low middleclass uneducated family. That girl's mother is a siren who has demented Manas. She is an adulterous woman.

Mother said;

I can't agree to your remarks. I have no daughter but her daughter is like my daughter. Manas is guilty. Why he entered into their trap.

Your choice for Manas's better half has all deserving and praise worthy virtues like beauty, glamour, higher education and status but Can you change his fate? Every thing depends on His order as marriages are made in heaven.

Manas couldn't defy his elder brother. He accompanied the negotiator to inspect the bride.They arrived at the bride's house at 11 A.M. the bride's parents, her brothers, her grandmother and a few beautiful women of their neighbours welcomed them with due hospitality . The bride named Suvasandhya was a very beautiful slim blonde. Her fair complexion was spotless. She was looking like a fairy. When she sat in front of Manas the women standing near doorstep whispered very nice match and giggled.

Manas smiled and asked;

What is your dream in life?

She said;

I am a big dreamer but who knows what is time's decree?

Manas said;

You may go now. I have nothing more to ask.

After bridal inspection manas and the negotiator ate sweets and snacks. They sipped tea and got ready to depart.

The women folk signalled the negotiator to their side and wanted to know opinion of Manas.

The negotiator came and asked him;

Do you choose the girl?

Manas said;

Give me one to two days for final decision.

The negotiator went inside and came out smiling to join him. God knows what he has said to them.

Manas think deeply about Shilpa's mother and found her matchless in her love trap. He couldn't help laughing when he remembered her tricks to tempt him for sex. He recollected the image of her pissing near a bush at her homestead land and signalling him to come and inspect the wet spot where she had pissed and laughed. Really she is very sweet. Her buttock, her pelvis, her toes, her thigh and her nipple are very seductive. He murmured;

I am going to marry shilpa, My sweet mother-in-law I can't part from you.

CHAPTER 3

Manas returned to his home with the negotiator. His elder brother took the negotiator to the rear side of their house. He talked with the negotiator in an inaudible voice for 10 to 20 minutes. When they came to front side of their house Manas and his mother were sitting in the sun rays to warm up . The negotiator was silent but his elder brother shouted in a commanding voice;

All family members of the girl are agree. So the marriage will take place within 15 days .I will visit the bride's house to finalise the date of marriage consulting with the astrologer. He also said that there were probably two dates of marriage in Biraja almanac within 15 days. He would like to choose the earliest date. He wouldn't wait for Manas's consent. He also clarified that he had sent Manas to inspect the bride as her family members wished for a meeting of the groom and bride before marriage. Hearing his brother's words Manas looked at his mother's face and found her very calm and reserved.

His elder brother went to attend Hare Krishna kirtan organised by a nearby villager on obsequies of his father. His middle brother also went out of home to purchase ration from the local grocer's shop. Manas's mother said to him;

You should return to your hostel in cuttack .If you stay here the situation will be more complex. You leave the house by afternoon. The amount necessary for your monthly hostel expenses has been arranged by selling rice. You tell your elder brother that you have an examination and convince him that you will do everything as to his guidelines. I will manage the situation here. I am always with you and pray God for your success and happiness. You should not betray the poor girl .

Manas became very happy. The portrait of his beloved and giggling of his sweet mother-in-law started reeling in his eyes. In a state of emotional delusion he felt touch of his mother-in-law. Her affectionate affinity and care for him , her sweet words, her waddling in front of him, her yellow coloured feet and toes and her slogging steps towards the bush in her homestead land for pissing became alive in his memories. His beloved's innocence, her dream and her surrender of virginity to him persuaded him to marry her. He analysed the difference between the dream land of opulence and the real land of joy and emotion.

After lunch Manas got ready to leave home. His elder brother gave 700 rupees to him for pocket expenses for a week and said;

Don't think of them. That woman is a siren. She is on her way to catch you in sex trap. After a week you come back. I am making all arrangements for your marriage. After marriage You will forget them and hate them. Manas nodded his head and went out of his home. When he touched his mother's feet he saw tears in her eyes and thought himself guilty. His mother wiped out her tears with skirts of her white saree and kept her hand on his head. Manas couldn't control his tears. After going a few steps forward he looked back and found his mother standing and looking at him. She had kept stone on her heart to part from her son. Perhaps she knew that Manas couldn't release himself from his mother-in- law's trap even after his marriage with her daughter. She will want him to stay with them and to get detached from his own family members. She is very shrewd to bewitch any young man with her coquettish gesture.

Instead of going to college hostel Manas arrived at his beloved's house. Seeing him Shilpa's mother came running to the threshold of her house and embraced him with all her force. She sent her daughters to the neighbour's house and pulled Manas to her lap. She went on kissing him for 5 minutes and wanted to know how he managed to come out of his elder brother's custody.

Manas looked at her and said;

I can't live without seeing you. You have demented me.

She laughed and said;

I knew that when you visited the wet spot where I had pissed. you can't forget me. You are going to be my dearest son-in-law.

She sat beside him and moved her grand toe on his feet. As he smiled she wanted him to tell her everything that happened at his house after their departure. Manas gazed at her toes polished with rosy nail enamel. She smiled and said;

You are dying for me. Isn't it? There is nothing new in my trick to make you chase like a male dog chases a bitch. When a bachelor sees naked fair organs of a woman for the first time he becomes mad to touch and play the game of sex. After first 5 years of marriage he loses interest in it and realises that as a bachelor he was a fool to feel that fair organ of a woman was the most valuable thing of life. I demented you and made you a fool. To test your foolishness I signalled you to visit the wet spot where I had pissed. You sat there , smelled the soil and pissed on that spot. Really you have become my slave. I knew that these words will have no meaning for you. I am not going to make you a fool as you are going to marry my daughter. Be happy with her and respect me as your mother-in –law.

Manas realised his blunder and nodded his head. At that time Shilpa and her sisters came to room. Manas narrated how he had gone to inspect a bride. Listening to his words Shilpa cried. Her mother said;

Why are you crying? He was forced to do so. He managed to pretend and came out of his elder brother's custody. You are going to marry to marry at puri tomorrow. As you are going to marry listen to my words;

Love in relationship and conjugal life are two different things. Marriage is not a child's play like doll's marriage. So pray God to make your married life happy and prosperous. Manas's mother has given her consent for marriage as she wants to see her son happy at the cost of her happiness.

Everybody became very happy. Shilpa's father consulted his younger brother who was staying at cuttack and finalised their tour to cuttack. Manas, Shilpa and her parents arrived at Cuttack in the evening. They purchased new paint and shirt for Manas and saree for Shilpa. They took rest for the night . On the next day morning they started journey to Puri in a hired car. Having arrived at Puri they purchased flower garlands, consulted a priest and performed marriage by exchange of garlands in front of Garuda Pillar. Manas put flower garland in Shilpa's neck and she put flower garland in Manas's neck. The priest chanted a few lines of hymns for Hindu marriage as per Gandharva marriage ritual.

Shilpa's parents were very poor. They couldn't afford for marriage at a marriage citadel in puri. Even they had no fund to hire a taxi from cuttack to their home. They travelled in a bus.

On the next day Shilpa's father visited Manas's house and invited them fourth night rituals of Manas and Shilpa. She gave her consent and arrived at Manas's father-in-laws house. She blessed her son and daughter-in-law in the following words.

Life is a challenge and those who retreat from challenge hardly realise worth of life. Both of you have to struggle to prove power of love. You have to establish yourself in the society. There is nobody to help you. May God guide you to the path of success and happiness.

Even today his mother's words echo in Manas's ear. Her blessings came true.

CHAPTER 4

Manas's wife Shilpa conceived a child. She communicated the message to Manas with a big smile on her face. He smiled and congratulated her. After while he became thoughtful as he had a little income from tuition. The extra burden of father hood was an ordeal for him. He pondered over the matter for a long time but didn't reveal his conflict of mind and heart to his wife.

It was 8.30 P.M. He was sitting on cot at his father-in-law's house. One and half year had passed from the date of his marriage . He thought of leaving his father-in-law's house after birth of a child. He didn't like the life of a domesticated son-in-law. Day to day the behaviour of his father-in –law and mother-in –law 's attitude was changing. They were poor men and unable to carry financial burden. His mother-in-law was no longer the same as she was before his marriage. Her selfishness was not a surprise for Manas, a post graduate student in English. It was going to sit for the final M.A examination after four months. So he suggested his wife to go for an abortion of the child in her womb. She didn't take it seriously .When Manas repeated the proposal of abortion she got angry and said;

Why are you making drama. Give me ten rupees to purchase coconut for Lord Siddheswar Mahadev. I will pray for a son.

Manas smiled and gave a ten rupees note to her hand. She touched that note at his forehead and handed over to her mother Shrimantini. She laughed and said;

My son-in-law, where is sweet? It is my due as your trainer.

Shilpa couldn't understand but laughed. Manas said;

You want sweets in advance to be trainer of our child. Shrimantini casted a coquettish gaze at his face, stood infront of him , kept her left hand between her two thighs and pressed her inner organ. She sent Shilpa to the kitchen for making tea.

Manas smiled and moved his head to and fro. She blinked at him and sat beside him. Four of them sipped tea. Manas said nothing and started reading a book . Shrimantini and her daughter went out of his room.

On the next day Manas and shilpa took bath and went to Shiva temple. They offered coconut and worshipped Lord Shiva. Both of them feel proud and happy. Returning from temple Manas found his mother-in-law murmuring something. She was unhappy as Manas and shilpa hadn't invited him to temple. Manas whispered to Shila;

Don't tell any thing. You go and prepare lunch. I am going to the local market. When Manas was going out of house Shrimantini called him from back and said;

Today is prathamastami.Take 100 rupees and purchase a Lungi and Ganjee for you.

Manas said;

I am not elder son of my parents. So there is no need of putting on new dress on prathamastami.

Shrimantini came close to Manas and put a hundred rupee note in his shirt packet. Manas went to the local market. He purchased a new saree for Shilpa. The cloth dealer said;

Shilpa is like my daughter. As you are going to be father it is the best occasion to gift her a new saree. It is the month of December, the month of Goddess Laxmi. So the occasion is very auspicious.

Manas paid 300 hundred rupees to the cloth dealer and returned back. He gave the new saree to Shilpa. She and her mother became very happy.

Her mother laughed and said;

You really prove that you are going to be father. Everybody celebrated the occasion. Shilpa put on new saree and took blessings. In that night Manas discussed with his wife how to increase his earnings. He said;

Ten months is not a very long time. After birth of child the expenditure will increase. Your monthly medical check up, medicines and expenses at the time of delivery need more money. So I am going to open a coaching centre. I have to invest a few hundreds for house rent and advertisement. I am going to print 10000 leaflets for distribution through news paper. So that the news of my coaching centre will reach to every house, mess and hostel near the Govt. college and Women's college of the local town.

Shilpa said;

Your teaching will definitely pull students in large numbers to our coaching centre. There wil be no loss.

Manas started his coaching centre. More and more students enrolled in the coaching centre. His income grew. He earned 10 to 12 thousand rupees per month and opened a pass book in the head post office of the town. He gave 2000 rupees to Shilpa for her hand expenses, spent 1000 for house rent , five hundred for his lunch and tiffin and deposited the rest amount in post office pass book. Every day he came from his father-in-law's house in the morning. After teaching to three groups of students he took lunch in the hotel and took rest in the coaching centre. Again he started teaching from 2PM to 5P.M and returned back to his father in law's house in the evening. His wife encouraged him to expand his coaching hours. Accordingly he taught another two groups in the evening and returned to home at 9 PM. After six months he became able to save 50 thousand rupees. Day to day his fame as very good teacher in English increased. He gave English coaching to all students starting from intermediate to post graduation students. He also gave coaching for spoken English.

His wife gave birth to a son. It was normal delivery. His wife gave him 15000 rupees that she had saved from her pocket expenses. Manas distributed sweets to the neighbours, to all students of coaching centre and spent 8000 rupees in the celebration of his son's naming ceremony on 21st days his birth. Manas's mother attended the ceremony. He purchased new clothes for his mother, mother-in- law , his sister-in-laws, son and for shilpa. They celebrated the function with pomp and splendour.

CHAPTER 5

Having spent two years of married life at his father-in-law's house Manas went to live at a rented house at local town Malatipur with his wife Shilpa and six months old son Ronak. As he had got nothing from his father-in-law's house he purchased everything such as bed stead, utensils, stove, electric fan, utensil stand, dining table, kitchen axe , knife , pressure cooker and all necessary household articles. It was a mixed experience of joy and pain of burden to arrange everything for a happy conjugal life. He spent more than 30 thousand in purchase of all necessary household appliances including T.V. The rented house had two bed rooms, one kitchen, a bathroom and very small space for keeping cycle or bike. I t was a new experience to live independently with wife and son. On the next day he purchased a lantern, two brooms, a strainer , a funnel , first aid box, cloth stand, iron screw, a small hammer , hangers and electric iron. In this way it took a whole day to purchase all essential articles.

In the evening his wife prepared a cup of hot tea. Her sister kabita was fondling Ronak. She arrived at their rented house in the evening to assist her sister. Manas was tired as he had spent the whole day in marketing. Sitting on bed stead he thought about the difference between joint family and nuclear family. In his child hood days he had seen the family members buying household goods from the local fair. Every member shared responsibility. They enjoyed leisure of merry making , visiting friends and relatives house. The nuclear family life in cities is very monotonous and burdensome. It is almost a slavery of domestic life for a husband. Being lost in thought he had forgotten to sip tea.

Seeing the tea cup full of tea Shilpa said to him;

You are lost in thought. You are gifted with amazing sensibility and puerile innocence.

Manas returned from his world of thought and said to his wife;

What is the matter? Have you made tea for me? .

Shilpa patted him and said;

I gave you hot tea before 20 minutes. As you were thinking some thing you couldn't notice it.Manas laughed and said;

You are right. I was engrossed in flash backs of our village life in childhood. You take the tea and make it hot .

Having drunk tea Manas went to the market and purchased mixture, biscuits and other dry snacks. when he came back he saw two sisters busy in making bread and curry for the night. His son Ronak was sleeping. He offered dry snacks to the hands of his sister-in-law kabita and told her to give parched rice mixed with mixture to him. While munching parched rice he listened to some old romantic songs on radio. He felt loneliness. The environment of his father-in-law's house was more joyous than living in a rented house with wife and son. Actually he was unhappy as he was missing Shrimantini, his mother-in-law. Her waddling inside the house with sounds of jingling bracelets on feet, the coquettish smile and leering were too sweet to forget. When he was listening to radio his wife shilpa said;

Your mood is off. I also feel unhappy. It feels so as we are new to this environment.

Kabita said;

Our mother, father and youngest sister Sabita would feel the same. We were living together for years. So all of us feel lonely here. Let us watch T.V .

Manas agreed with them. He slept in bed and kabita pressed his feet. After watching T.V for an hour they ate and went to bed. Kabita and Shilpa slept in a room and he slept in another room. While listening song on radio he slept. In dream he saw Shrimantini embracing and kissing him. He woke up, opened the door of shilpa's room and beckoned her to come. Kabita was snoring. Shilpa came out of room and closed the door very slowly. Manas took her to his chest, switched of the light and enjoyed her. After half an hour she went to sleep with kabita and her little son Ronak. Manas closed his eyes and slept.

CHAPTER 6

Time rolled on. Manas got settled at Malatipur town and became popular as a very resourceful teacher in English. Every day hundreds of students came to him for tuition in English. He made 8 to 10 groups for themas there were students from intermediate to post graduate. He took a big house on rent which had three bed rooms, one big drawing room, big dinning space, kitchen, two latrines and very spacious portico. Every month Shrimantini visited his rented house and spent a few days with them. Five years passed, Manas became a well to do man of the town. His wife Shilpa was going to give birth to her second child. Manas's mother arrived at his rented house and stayed for a few months. She became happy to see her son's prosperity. Manas had joined in a private college as lecturer in English. He had name, fame and status. His house was repleted with costly furnitures, colour TV, fridge and sofa. He had purchased a new scooter. He had land line telephone and LPG cylinder. He maintained luxurious life.

His mother's presence at his residence made him very happy. His mother said;

My blessings are always with you. You will reach the apex of success. Goddess Saraswati would never desert you. Where ever you will seat, you will earn money. You brothers are unhappy. You ought to give money to them in every month. They are cultivating land and working hard. They can enjoy the joy of purchasing groceries , snacks and nutrient food items for their children.

Shilpa objected to her proposal and said;

Why shall we give money? They refused to accept me and my little son. I had gone to stay with them. If they had allowed me to live with them they would have got money every month. There would have no necessity of double expenses and a big rented house. We are not taking rice from home. His college hasn't got grant-in-aid of Govt. He is working hard to earn money. Giving coaching to 8 to 10 groupes of students in a day is very strenuous task.They are reaping crops, fishes from two ponds, mangoes of 30 to 40 trees, selling bamboos, tamarind , coconut, pine apple and bananas.

She further said to her mother-in-law;

Mother, we have duty and obligation for you. Wee will be happy if you live with us forever. I find no logic to back up your elder sons who hardly think of us and send anything from home.

Mother listened to her and said;

Manas was a small boy when his father died. His elder brother has taken care of him and his education. So you should contribute a little money for his children as a token of gratitude and payment of loan.

Shilpa had too narrow mind and eccentric heart to endorse mother's gust of impartial sagacity. Manas and his middle brother had gone to market to purchase fish. Having returned from market he heard everything from his mother and became very sad at heart. His wife Shilpa was an average matriculate girl of a poor family . She hadn't learnt culture of humility and gratitude. Very often he found her very selfish and commercial in her approach to relationship. She was also reluctant to spend for her sisters. So Manas tried to make her realise Shilpa's ignorance and lack of proper education.

His mother said;

I have nothing to blame her. Whatever she told is based on sum of life of post modern society. She was not with you in your past. Your brothers were with you. So you have to teach her the essence of good relationship. Wealth, happiness and progress can't go together unless you share your earnings for wants and pleasure of your kindreds, benefactors and well wishers.

Shilpa overheard the conversation between mother and son. She was about to throw her reaction but Manas beckoned her to be silent. She fumed and went to kitchen for cooking.

It was 2P.M. Manas, his middle brother , his mother, shilpa and his sister-in-law kabita sat together for lunch. The local passenger train from Malatipur to his village was at 3,30 P.M. His middle brother got ready to catch train. Manas started his scooter to carry him to railway station. He gave a five hundred note to his middle brother but he wanted more. Mother was standing near them. Watching them Shilpa said in an irritated voice;

We are staying outside in the rented house. We are purchasing everything , even water as we have to pay the electric bill for enjoying water supply. You are living in the village. You can manage any situation taking help of your village people and relatives. Who will help us? It is town life. Our next door neighbour is a stranger to us. So receive the amount gladly whatever is given to you for snacks of the children at our village home.

His middle brother smiled and said;

You are right but loss of Rabi crops has put us in problem. Total 6 acres of paddy was lost due to lack of water. Scanty rain fall and failure of Govt. deep well made the paddy plants dead. That is why we are facing problem to invest for kharif crops and to maintain grocery and vegetable requirements of the family.

Manas had bought ration for the month before two days. So he told Shilpa to pack 2 packets of mustard oil, biscuits and some other grocery items in a bag .He gave that bag to his brother and both of them went to railway station in his scooter.

Their mother was standing on the door step. She folded her hands and offered prayer to God for safe journey of her sons.

Manas returned to his residence at 4 PM after leaving his middle brother in the train compartment. He dropped his scooter speedily to attend a group of tuition students waiting at his residence. His mother was gossiping with the tuition students and enjoying their remarks about Manas ability as a teacher in English. When Manas started teaching all students said in one voice

"Sir, your mother is a very fine motherly figure with a lots of information starting from legends to current affairs. Manas laughed and said I always believed that our fore fathers teaching about social relationship are a great lesson for time to come. They had said it rightly that wealth, prosperity and happiness cannot go together, if we fail to share our earnings and time for our kindreds, benefactors and well wishers when they want our sharing, Mother is an embodiments of rich heritage and continuation of Hindu culture that is the oldest and the richest culture of the world. Do you not feel proud of being borne in India, the land of God & Goddess, saints, Holi rivers, Priests and wondering monk and ascetics. Now Manas realised that perhaps he was going out of the realm of the students understanding level. He smiled and said alright, my brothers and your mothers are the breads of the same soil and deserve our respect. I am happy that you have spent some moments with my mother. Let us start a lesson from your prose book about India the land and the people by writer S. Donald Connery. Though this topic is in the last serial of your prescribed syllabus for the year, but a thought it proper to teach it today as you as well as my mother will be happy to know that how the foreigners have deep regards for Indian culture, love of tradition and craze for co-sharing of Indian festivals that go all along the year with flying colours of high expectation mirth and joy.

The foreigners those who have share intimate moments with the Indian have realised how the Indians have cheese like pure heart and mercury like fleeting mind. They are easily delighted and get depressed at the very next moment when something go beyond their expectation. It is a peculiar fact that the Indian writers who have got man booker prize by publishing their books in United Kingdom have not highlighted rich heritage of India rather they have vituperated Indian culture to pocket the award that is meant for the books published from the publishers of United Kingdom. On the other hand, the English writer like T.S Eliot,and W B Yeats and many more have highly eulogised Indian way life and got Noble prize in literature.

Some of the students wanted to know why such things happen ? Why the Indian writers get their book published from United Kingdom and criticised Indian culture in their contents. Manas was about to say something but his Mother stopped him and said the answer is very simple. The Britishers and the Moguls ruled over India for 500 years. Many invaders looted precious jewels and statues from our Country . How did they become able to do so. They gave some appellations like Rai Sardar, Rai Bahadur, Baliar Singh, Bhuj Bal and many such alluring titles and foreign gifts to draw our native Kings and conscious intelligentsia to their fold. We the Indians are too selfish and too craze for award, reward and undue praise. The students clapped their hands and Manas said " the whole discussion was not a tale about the Indians tell-tale nature, but the very real purport of the writer Connery"s observation on Indian life and Indians in the topic India the land and the people. Your tuition time is over, you go and let me visit the Bal Gopal temple taking Mother with me as she is fond of visiting temple in the evening.

It was about 7.30 PM, Manas took his Mother to the Bal Gopal temple situated at Kachery Bazar of Malatipur town. When mother stepped in to the temple, she moved around deeply observing the engraved statues of rasa of Lord Krishna from child hood to the King of Dwarika. Manas set on the temple premises and watched her mother activities as an infant learner of ABCD alphabets of theology. Mother set inside the temple, closed her eyes, lifted her hands and tears rolled down from her checks. Perhaps she was completely drenched with devotion or sharing the real pathos of child Krishna's departure for Gopapur in the chariot of Ugrashen to fight with demon Kansha. When she opened her eyes and prostrated before the deity her mode changed, Manas found a big smile on her face while receiving Basil leaf and ambrosia from the temple priest.

Manas smiled but told nothing as he knew that realisation, perception, apperception and introspection are the products of growing as experience and expertise. His mother came out of the temple and told him that she wanted to buy an iron mortar. She also said that the iron mortar that was at his village home was over size for use in all purpose. She wanted to buy a middle size iron mortar. Manas took her to Mr Sens Hardware store located at the purlieu of Bal Gopal temple. Having purchased the iron mortar, Manas said to his mother

"Do you want anything more to purchase, let us go and purchase a shoe for you, she smiled and said, I purchased the iron mortar not for me, but for one of my village friend who visits Lord Jagannath temple everyday with me in the evening and shared her pathetic stories of domestic displeasure. Her daughter-in-law is an arrogant lady of bellicose temperament. She tortures her mother-in-law beyond toleration. She needs the mortar to churn betalnut and pan leaf as she is teeth less. Manas and his mother returned back. His mother watched some religious serials on TV and fondled his son Ronak. His wife, Shilfa cooked food and his sister-in-law assisted her. They enjoyed supper at 10.30 PM. Mother went to her bed and started preparing beetle leaf to chew, Manas set by her side and wanted to know from her the happenings at his village as he had not gone to village for 8 to 10 months. He had gone during Durga Puja and the next year's Durga Puja was 2-3 months ahead. His mother put the beetle leaf in her mouth, munched it and said to Manas

"I have forgotten to tell a shameless incident that happened in your Jintendra uncle' house. Manas said what happened to him? He was staying at Balasore with his wife where the incident took place ? whether at Balasore or at his father-in-law's house. Mother said as you know, his wife Lilabati was a capricious lady of extra modern gay nature, she used to spend maximum days at her father's house. Your Jitender uncle was perhaps a mismatch for her. The marriage took place in an as usual way of arranged marriage. Lilabati's

father was an ex land lord undivided Balasore and Medna Pur district. As your Jitendra uncle joined as SDO in Telecommunication of BSNL company. He purchased the groom for her wayward daughter. It happened and nobody objected to such mismatch arranged marriage. The matter became worst when her adulterous nature crossed all borders. She ran away with a Muslim driver leaving her two children at home. Manas called his wife Shilpa to share the story how the incident took place and why Jitendra uncle let the things fall apart.

Jitendra got marriage at the age of 35. After getting a Govt job. His wife Lilabati was the eldest among 5t daughter of Natabar Dhall, the ex land lord of Unida province. Litabati was 12 years junior to Jitendra when marriage took place before 15 years. She had a 12 years son and 9 years old girl. They were staying in a rented house at Naya Bazar, Balasore. A muslim was a driver of BSNL company and he was engaged as a Driver of your uncle, so everyday he visited your uncle's house took his sons and daughter to School, purchased necessary rations, apart from his official duty. Lilabati developed illicit love affair with that muslim driver 3 to 4 years before. Jitendra came to know about the matter, but preferred to be a wittol. Actually he was not so up-to-date to fulfil demands of his beautiful wife like shopping, touring fair or watching Opera. He was engrossed in his official work and thought that the object of his marriage was fulfilled as he had become father of two children. He did not care for his wife desires and motives. It gave ample chance to Lilabati to be a wench. She went away with the muslim driver Mr Nazidullaha and spent a few weeks in Kolkata. They returned back to Balasore after one and half month. Your uncle had nothing objection to accept her, but his family members and colleagues slenderer him calling him an eunuch. So, remained silent and sent his wife to his father-in-law's house. Six months passed. One day, he took help of our village people and raided her house to bring back his nine years old daughter who had gone to live with her after her return to Kolkata. A physical tussle took place between your uncle's father-in-law, his

followers and our village people. The police brought two groups to Police Station for an amicable settlement. To the utter surprise of the villagers, Jitendra signed on the agreement that he had nothing objection to his wife's conduct. The villagers found the matters very shameless and returned back.

Having listened to the story, Manas said to his mother " do you feel that their family life will be enjoyable after this ugly incident. Mother laughed and said this is life and its unexpected term with multiple options. Their life was not enjoyable at the beginning and they had not tried to make that enjoyable. The matte is how may learn from such faults and attempt for removing impurities of sinister force spoiling significance of life. Manas's wife wanted to know from her mother-in-law who was to be blamed for the ugly happening. Manas was looking at his mother's face expecting a very befitting answer from which Shilfa would learn something. His mother asked Shilfa according to your judgement who is the guilty, Shilpa said Jitendra uncle is more guilty than his wife. Why he took it granted that an educated daughter of a ex Land lord would be satisfied with him just for his designation. Every woman has their personal choice and physical urge. Nothing can barricade a woman's desire for love, when the husband remains indifferent to her. Mother smiled and said, good, but conjugal life is a matter of the function of two hand. We cannot clap in one hand. We cannot talk without presence of somebody, we cannot celebrate when others are not joining with us, In the same way, Jitendra and Lilabati both were indifferent to each other. As a result, such a domestic derangement happened. Manas and Shilpa nodded their head and went to sleep. Mother closed her eyes folded her hands, uttered "Hari Omm" and went to sleep.

CHAPTER 7

His mother stayed with them for three months to attend on Shilpa's second delivery. It was evening of first October. His wife felt delivery pain. He wanted to admit her in the nursing home. His mother wanted the same but Shilpa wanted to go to her father's house. Her first delivery was a normal delivery at her father's house. There was a mid wife named Hema who was very more competent than any trained nurse. She had record of making hundreds delivery successful. So Shilpa was confident that her second delivery would be a normal delivery at home. She had the apprehension that the doctor at nursing home would unnecessarily go for scissoring only for their profit. Manas and and his mother tried their best to convince her that if any problem arises they would face difficulty to bring her to nursing home at Malatipur town. They ought not go from Malatipur town to her father's house in the village. Generally the delivery patients come to town to avail of medical facility. She would be considered a fool to leave her town residence. Shilpa didn't listen to their suggestion and refused to go to any nursing home or hospital for delivery. So his mother suggested him to hire an auto rickshaw. She accompanied shilpa in that auto rickshaw to her father's house. Manas took his son Ronak and sister-in-law kabita in his scooter. They reached at Shilpa's house at 8.30 P.M. Her excruciating delivery pain started at 11 P.M. They called for Hema and she arrived. She said;

Everything will be right. The delivery is going to happen within 2 to 3 hours. Manas and his mother sat at the drawing room and prayed God for smooth and safe delivery. Shilpa's mother assisted Hema and her father was sitting at his bed room. All of them were waiting to listen cry of the new born infant. Time rolled on. She howled in severe pain. It was going to be 3.30 P.M. Everybody became worried. Even Hema lost her confidence. So Manas started his journey in scooter to Malatipur town for hiring a vehicle to carry Shilpa to Nursing Home. He was on the way and was about one kilometre away from Malatipur town he received cell phone call that an infant was born. He thanked God and returned back as fast as he could. Arriving at his father-in-law's house, he heard cries of the new born infant echoing from the room. He came to know that Shilpa had given birth to a son. It was a moment of inarticulate mental relief and joy. As he entered into the drawing room of his father-in-law's house, his sister-in-law, midwife Hema and a few women of the neighbourhood congratulated him and demanded sweets. Hema came out of the room and said give me 5 thousand rupees which you might have spent in the Nursing Home. I have the experience of making more than 100 delivery successful. You made me nerves, so I remained silent when you started your scooter and went out to hire a vehicle. At that moment I was sure that the child would come out from her womb within 10 to 15 minutes. Manas laughed and said really all praise fall short of your practical knowledge and confidence. I and my mother became worried as we had concerned for life of the mother as well as the baby in the womb. My mother said to Hema, as time passed and excruciating pain became intolerable, we became worried. You remained calm as you had knowledge and expectancy in the matter. Hema smiled and said I am not going to blame you rather I have respect for your kind heart and affection. I have seen many mothers who are callous to the sufferings of their daughter-in-laws. From the very beginning you were telling that you want safety of mother and the baby. The safety of the mother is more precious. I would share your example with others when situations would warrant me to do so. Very often it is found that the mother-in-laws object to taking their daughter-in-law to Nursing home for delivery. For them money matters but not lives. Manas's mother laughed and said your service for the mother and infant is praiseworthy. You are doing a very noble work by helping the delivery patient of countryside. The remuneration that you take in shape of a new saree and sweets is not the remuneration, but a sundry gift. All of them laughed and celebrated the occasion.

CHAPTER 8

The pace of life and path of aging process bring forth the risk of taking many responsibility on the shoulder. The situation stands sometime conducive and sometime contrary but the call of duty as to the call of our and bare need is not a matter to be avoided. Manas took the charge of finding out bridegroom for his sister-in-law Kabita's marriage. At that time, very often his elder brother, a few friends and some people of his father-in-law's village advised him not to take extra responsibility. There were of the view that he had sacrificed a lot by marrying one of their daughter without diary and compromising the social level of education and economic status. One of his father-in-law neighbour a school teacher called Manas for sharing of tea at his house and said you belong to a good family and post graduate in English, you have already sacrificed a lot for the family of your father-in-law. Now a days, the brothers are taking risk of marriage of their sisters, why shall you take the risk of finding bridegroom and managing expenses of marriage of your sister-in-law. We know that as you are staying at Malatipur town and lecturer in profession, you can purchase vehicle and gold in credit, but you have to pay for moths together. Your father-in-law will shirk from economic obligation as it was the case with you. They did not give you even a vehicle or gold chain. As you got marriage, you lost the claim. Manas preferred meaningful silence to long sharing of limericks, he thanked that school teacher and said the call of responsibility and duty is not scaled and matted in the same way and in the same method. So, let me think over the matte,

Manas knew that his father-in-law and mother-in-law were not the man of affluence. They were of lower middle class standard and too weak to carry burden of holding marriage of 4 daughters. It was a part of their inability but not their reluctance to give gifts to any son-in-law, so Manas was confident that the relationship and dependence are inseparable. In relationship, those who are week, they usually became dependent on others who are a little more well off than them, so, how can he shirk from social obligation and morality. One incident cannot wash out or wipe out the blunder that one deliberately do, so, as to shirk benefit or to shirk from duty. Every matter leaves on indelible mark whether that was ought or ought not, the think never went to happen whether someone is going to extent his support or not.

While analysing the reels of live pertaining to his involvement in selection of bridegroom for his sister-in-law, one incident became very alive and wanted elaboration. He had gone with a negotiator to the house of the groom at village Krushnapur. The groom was working in Gujrat. The negotiator told that the groom was MA in Political science and was teacher in a international convent school. During inspection of the groom, Manas asked a few questions in a friendly way to be sure of the guy's qualification and personality. The first question was you are Post Graduate in which subject, the groom said, I am MA and post graduate, than Manas asked sorry, you are MA in which subject. The groom said in MIL, English, History, Political Science, Logic and Sanskrit. Manas asked from which University you got all the MA degrees. The groom said I degree from our local college and working in Gujrat. The negotiator was laughing as he thought the groom was giving answers to Manas's very smartly. The negotiator was an illiterate schedule cast middle aged man who had nothing knowledge about educational qualification. Manas rejected that groom telling that he was not satisfied with the groom's personality. The negotiator said you may or may not give your sister-in-law in marriage with him but you cannot deny his fluency in English. He went to the extent of telling that the groom was more fluent in English the than British officers.

After one and half years of persistence search for the groom, finally Manas became able to find out a suitable groom for his sister-in-law, the groom was a third grade employee of Govt in the department of Revenue. He had 3 brothers, two elder brothers were out of the state with their families. His widow mother was getting pension, he was the youngest among the 3 brothers. The young man was handsome, humble and gentle in behaviour. The betrothal took place within a week and marriage date was fixed. It was a great relief for Manas who realised that searching for a good groom was an ardours task. He thanked God for giving him a chance to experiences multiple problems in his youth. Only 15 days were left for marriage. He took the whole charge of marketing as well as consulting the tent house, cook, drummers, fire crackers, Brahmin, barber and floweriest. His wife Shilpa cooperated with him. Every day the wife and the husband spent 3 to 4 hours roaming here and there at local town Malatipur to give concrete shape to all arrangements. It took almost 8 to 10 days to complete the whole arrangement.

On the day of marriage, it rained very heavily. 1 quintal of mutton curry and other items of both veg and non-veg dishes for 500 people were cooked, due to rain and storm, the procession was obstructed. Previously they had told to arrange food for 200 people in the bridegroom's procession, but actually that reduced to one forth. Even the drum beater, fire cracker dealer could not display their entertainment programme. It rained like cats and dogs till morning. However, marriage took place peacefully. The 50 to 60 people who accompanied the bridegroom were almost half drenched having taken their meal they hurriedly returned back in the vehicle meant for them. The cook suggested to arrange a fist for the neighbours in the morning to avoid wastage of cooked mutton curry and other veg and non-veg items.

3

ADULTHOOD

CHAPTER 1

Manas's sister-in-law faced problem to cope with her drunkard husband. Her husband spent lavishly for his drunkard group and got victim of financial crisis. His extravagant nature increased day to day. Kabita tried her best to take him back from the wrong path but failed. His other brothers were also habitual drunkards. She consulted her father and Manas how to handle the unsocial, wayward and unworthy husband. Manas told her to have patience as he believed that the things would change after birth of a child. Years rolled on. She gave birth to a son. On 21days celebration of their first child Deepak Manas said to Kabita's husband;

Dear brother-in –law you are the father of a son. Don't squander your salary money for temporary pleasure of drinking sand feasting. Nobody denies you to enjoy life but enjoy it in company of your family members and spend money for the right purpose. You have liberty to spend your salary but at the same time you have responsibility tolook after your family and to save a little for future. The way of squandering hard earned money would definitely put you in problem to look after your family properly. So try to keep distance from drunkard friends and stop spending money for them like pouring water. When purse is full such friends usually flock but hid themselves at the time of your adversity.

He listened to Manas's words of real experiences and agreed with him. He also promised to amend his ways of life. Manas believed in him and thought that the affection for son and love for beautiful loyal wife would pull him back from aberration. There would be no passion for bawdy pleasure.

On his way back from Kabita's house Manas discussed the matter with his mother-in-law and she became very happy. After a week another incident at Kabita's house upset every body. Her husband forcibly took away gold neck lace and mortgaged that with the local liquor shop owner. He had taken liquor of worth 15thousand on credit from that shop and shared with his drunkard friends. That shopkeeper had seized his bike. He mortgaged his wife's gold necklace to release his bike. At the time of snatching necklace from her neck there was a violent encounter between wife and husband. He had injured her thrashing with a stick.

She telephoned to Shilpa and cried to come to her parents' house. Manas went to his father-in-law's house taking Shilpa with him .They discussed the matter and decided to take her fro his company. Accordingly he visited Kabita's house. At that time her husband Kumuda was sleeping. His mother was cooking and Kabita was sitting at rear side of her house. She was sobbing . She had injuries in her hands , palms and legs. Manas took permission of

Kumuda's mother and took her with her son from their house. He had no scope to talk with Kumuda as he sneaked from the sight.

Kabita stayed at her parents's house for a week. Kumuda didn't come to visit her. After 10 days he faced a road accident and got admitted in the district head hospital at Malatipur. One of his friend broke the news of his accident to Kabita over telephone. The district head hospital was 5 kilometre away from kabita's parental house. Having arrived at hospital Kabita and her parents called for Manas and Shilpa. Seeing everybody congregated Kumuda cried and said to Manas;

Brother forgive me.God saved me from death. Being over drunk I collided bike with an electric poll.

Manas sat beside him and said;

Don't be emotional and nervous. We are your well wishers. I feel that your wife's good luck and good works saved your life. God wants you to be a good husband and a responsible loving father for your son.

Kumuda spent 5 days in hospital bed. Kabita attended on him. Being discharged he went to Kabita's house. They spent two days and returned back to their house.

After that accident he parted with the habit of drinking liquor with his friends for a week. Kabita thought that her days of suffering came to an end. She communicated the good news to Manas and her sister Shila. They became very glad at Kabita's happy married life.

In the meanwhile Kumuda got transfer order and joined on duty at Rasgovind pur. When he loaded his furniture and other household goods in a truck to take from rented house at Khaira the local shop keepers did not allow him to take goods without giving payment for credits taken from them. He had taken credit from different shops in shape of goods and cash. He had to pay more than 50 thousands towards credit and interest on money taken from them. A money lender claimed 30 thousand from him. So everybody gathered in front of his rented house and obstructed his shifting of goods. His widow mother and kabita requested them to give time for payment of loans but they disagreed . Kabita intimated the problem TO Manas over telephone and he shared the matter with his father-in- law.

Manas and kabita's father arrived at Kumuda's rented house at Khaira at 3 P.M. The truck loaded with furniture and goods was standing in front of that rented house. Three men were sitting on chair at fdoor step of the rented house. Kumuda, his mother, his son and kabita were sitting inside the room. They were hungry. They had packed all household goods and had been waiting for 3 hours to leave.

Manas went to the nearby hotel and bought meals for them. He and his father-in- law gave payment to the local shop keepers and money lenders.

All of them went in the car to Rasgovindpur. Having unloaded all house hold goods and giving payment to the truck driver Manas gave 5 thousand rupees to kabita to meet immediate expenses. He and his father-in-law came back to Malatipur.

CHAPTER 2

Manas's family was an ideal happy family. His eldest son Ronak started his school education at Saraswati Shishu Mandir , Naya bazaar. His youngest son Rohit had taken admission in carmel covent School. Day to day his income from tuition was growing. He had nothing tension except the disturbances in his sister-in-law's married life. Nothing change took place in attitude and habit of kumuda. His family condition went from bad to worse. Kabita had given birth to another son. Her eldest son was 8 years old and the youngest son was 5 years old. Altercation among wife and husband had became an every day affair. Her 15 years of married life was full of displeasure and discontentment. Her drunkard husband Kumuda ruined the family life. They were living in acute poverty and debt. Manas and his father-in-law very often helped Kabita with money, groceries and rice bags. Oneday her husband sold his bikefor 5 thousand rupees. He had drunk countryside liquor from Natua Sial's shop on credit. He took away kumuda's bike as he couldn't pay 5 thousand rupees. This news agitated Manas. After getting the news Manas went to Natia Sial's house and saw Kumuda drinking country liquor at his verandah. He was absent from duty at office for six months and was roaming here and there drinking and feasting with friends, He had mortgaged all furnitures, TV, fridge and ornaments to meet his expenses.He was almost a pauper. Though he saw Manas he connived and looked at the opposite direction to avoid eye contact ..Manas said to Kumuda;

Come with me. Let us go to your house. There we will discuss how to get your bike back. I will help you.

Kumuda said;

I don't need anybody's help. I have given my bike to Nitia's son. They are my relatives. I am happy as they are giving snacks and liquor to me. It is not your college that you will give lecture to me. You are going to college to take one or two classes. You have money and leisure. That is why you are interfering with my family affairs. You go otherwise I will call Nitia's son to beat you. Who informed you that i have given my bike to Nitia's son Madhab who is reading in college. I have no doubt that Kabita has informed you. She is not my wife. Really she is your wife.

Listening to all such nonsense Manas lost his temper and slapped on Kumuda's cheeks. He dragged him out of Nitia's verandah and forcibly took him to his house . The distance was nearly 100 metres. His mother and Kabita supported Manas and scolded him. He scolded every body using filthy language. Kabita locked him inside a room. Manas, Kabita and kumuda's mother went to Nitia's house. Manas paid all his outstanding dues on kumuda and took bike from his house. He locked the bike and gave key to Kabita. He told her to unlock Kumuda.

Manas returned back to his house and reported everything to his wife Shilpa. She intimated the matter to her parents. In the evening Shilpa's parents arrived at her house and became very unhappy to know about Kumuda's false allegation against Manas.

Shilpa said;

Who is going to take a drunkard's allegation seriously. He would bark like a dog.

Shilpa's parents thanked him and returned back. Just after a month another incident took place in Kabita's house. Kumuda injured his mother and wife when they refused to give him key of the bike. When his neighbours congregated at his house he shouted in loud voice;

My wife has illicit relation with her brother-in-law, Manas , a lecturer in English who is living at Malatipur town. I am going to drive out such a bitch from my house. She might kill me. She is informing all personal affairs of our family to Manas. They are sinking in love.

The congregated neighbours took pity on Kabita and sent her with two sons to her parents house by an auto rickshaw. After returning from college Manas came to know the matter from his wife Shilpa. He laughed and said;

The day I slapped on Kumuda's cheeks and dragged him from his place of drinking liquor I was sure that he would make a drama to blame me.On that day he was making such nonsense allegation but hadn't taken the matter seriously as he was in a state of complete inebriation.

In that evening Manas and his wife went to meet kabita. His father-in-laws decided not to send kabita to Kumuda's house. Manas and his wife supported the idea because of danger to her life. Her two children were barely in need of nutrient food, care and peaceful environment. So kabita stayed in her father's house. Just after a week Kumuda came to take her back. He was looking like a skeleton without food and care. Kabita and her parents suggested him to stay with them and to attend the office regularly. He agreed to do so. Though he stayed at his father-in-law's house he didn't part from the habit of drinking. He

told lies that he was attending office. Everyday he came from his father-in-law's house and spent the office hour in company of drunkards near the liquor shop at Malatipur.

He surrendered one LIC Policy and gave Twenty seven thousand to Kabita telling that the amount was his salary money. He also told that he had spent three thousand for his journey from Malatipur town to his office . Kabita and her parents became happy . After two days Kumuda's mother informed that he had taken one LIC policy paper and surrendered that policy before maturity. One drunkard of his village was with Kumuda when he received thirty thousand from LIC office at Malatipur. He spent three thousand on drinking and eating mutton meal with drunkard friends at hotel.

Hearing the news his father-in-laws consulted with Manas and Shilpa for final decision about Kabita's future. Manas suggested to wait and tolerate Kumuda at least for a week before taking final decision.

Day to day kumuda became wild. He made friendship with drunkards of Kabita's village. He had another policy bond paper in his bag. One day he took that LIC policy bond paper and availed a loan of twenty thousand. He spent the whole amount on drinking and feasting with drunkards. He even spent nights with them. He drunk and bickered with his wife and father-in-laws.

After a week Shilpa's parents called for her with Manas and they decided to send Kumuda to his home. Accordingly they said to kumuda;

You might die from intake of excess alcohol. Why shall we take the risk? You go to your home and drink as much as you can.

Packing his clothes in a bag he went out. One of Kabita's village guy also went with him in his bike. Leaving kumuda at his home that guy returned back.

Three weeks passed. Kumuda's neighbours were giving all reports about his inebriated pandemonium at village. He got an opportunity when the campaign begun for Sarpanch election. He joined in campaigns of different candidates and drunk liquor day and night. He stayed in their village club house and shared opium, marijuana and countryside liquor up to his throat. He spent nights with a group of drunkards in hanging posters and banners of different candidates. In one morning his village people saw his dead body inside the nearby river. His face and head and chest was inside water and the rest part of his body was on soil at the brink of riverbed. It was the month of February. Manas was on duty at college when his father-in-law broke out the news to him at 12.30 P.M. Hearing the news he arrived at the district head hospital where Kabita, her two sons, her parents, Kumuda's mother, her elder son and many people of her village including the ex-Sarpanch were present. Every body was waiting for taking his dead body from hospital after post mortem. It was a heart breaking sight. Kabita and her sons were crying. A few drunkard want-wits of kumuda's village were scolding Kabita accusing her of neglecting her husband. They told that as Kabita stayed in her father's house Kumuda couldn't tolerate separation from his wife. He drank day and night and finally died from excess intake of alcohol. They also said that kumuda might had gone to river bed to attend call of nature early in the morning. As he was over drunk his feet slipped and he fell down into river water. As his nose got sunk inside water he couldn't respire and died.

Those caddish fellows were abusing kabita using unrefined language. Every body was silent. Manas objected to such nonsense comments and requested the ex-Sarpanch to dissuade them from such antisocial behaviour. The ex- Sarpanch scolded them and made them silent. The situation went in favour of Kabita. The village people praised her patience and sufferings at the hands of an irresponsible drunkard husband for 15 years.

Kabita, her two sons and her parents went to kumuda's house to attend cremation. The ex- sarpanch made all arrangements and helped kabita, her sons and her parents to return back to their house after completion of cremation.

Manas , shilpa and their two sons were waiting for their arrival. They had locked the rented house at Malatipur. They spent the sleepless night consoling kabita. Manas and shilpa assured her of all kinds of help and care. Her parents declared to record their home stead land and property in her name. She will be rehabilitated in her husband's post. Manas made her sure of getting Govt. service in place of her husband. He took the whole responsibility of making all official works for her posting and said to her;

Life is a living school of learning. It invites for facing the unexpected with hope and patience. That is why life is a zest for living despite ups and downs, joy and sorrow.

CHAPTER 3

Manas had committed a blunder in his life whwn he joined as a lecturer in English in a private college and continued his service hoping that he would get grant-in- aid as to the then standing grant-in- aid policy of providing one third of the salary after 5 years of service in a private college, two third after 7 years and full salary after 9 years. Nothing of that sort happened. The then congress Govt. in Odisha broke that grant-in aid policy and forgot its duty towards higher education. 14 years went from the date of his joining in the college. The secretary of governing body of the college was giving 500 rupees salary to every teaching staff and that was not regular. His earning from coaching was enough to sustain family. His sundry salary was the cost of fuel expenses for his scooter for 10 days. He had to spend earnings from coaching to attend college for a month. In those there was no govt. appointments in colleges for .a decade. He had no scope of trying for any other govt. jobs. His family burden had increased. As a father of two children he was focussing on more earnings from tuition to maintain comfortable living in the rented house at Malatipur town. He was busy with group coaching at his rented house from morning to 9 P.M . except a few hours in the college.

All lay men were in the governing body of the college like spices dealer, vegetable seller, village ward member, Sarpanch and petty politicians of the localty. They had hardly any knowledge of education. So the secretary was extorting money from students and considered the college as his personal business hub. Most of the members were illiterates. The defects in odisha education policy for opening of new colleges and absolute autonomy to the governing body of such colleges are cancerous to the basic norms of holistic education. The petty politicians of every political party opened colleges in their locality and got permission and affiliation. Most of the secretaries were taking financial donations from lectures and employees while giving appointments. Hardly they give salaries but defalcated the collection of rupees from students for admission. Readmission, tuition fees and public donations for development.

Manas and his college staff became unhappy when the governing body appointed a retired primary school teacher as principal of the college. When the staff tried to convince them that the governing body can't impose any outsider as principal of a recognised and affiliated educational institution. The boorish secretary said;

It is our college. The governing body has absolute power to appoint any body, to suspend or to dismiss any body in service. you have to work under the principal appointed by us.

That retired primary school teacher was a petty politician of a political party. He was out and out a mischief monger and corrupted man. He had been twice arrested for stealing pulses meant for students and defalcating public fund in construction of school building. His track record as a school teacher was very abboherent. The most nasty aspect of his personality was his sadist and lewd nature. All staff of the college opposed that tired school teacher's appointment as principal of the college. Manas was secretary of the staff association. So he took active role in strike against the illegal and unhustified decision of the governing body.

He met secretary of the governing body and tried his best to convince him that the appointment of a school teacher as principal of the financial donations from lectures and employees while giving appointments. Hardly they give salaries but defalcated the collection of rupees from students for admission. Readmission, tuition fees and public donations for development.

Manas and his college staff became unhappy when the governing body appointed a retired primary school teacher as principal of the college. When the staff tried to convince them that the governing body can't impose any outsider as principal of a recognised and affiliated educational institution. The boorish secretary said;

It is our college. The governing body has absolute power to appoint any body, to suspend or to dismiss any body in service. you have to work under the principal appointed by us.

That retired primary school teacher was a petty politician of a political party. He was out and out a mischief monger and corrupted man. He had been twice arrested for stealing pulses meant for students and defalcating public fund in construction of school building. His track record as a school teacher was very abboherent. The most nasty aspect of his personality was his sadist and lewd nature. All staff of the college opposed that tired school teacher's appointment as principal of the college. Manas was secretary of the staff association. So he took active role in strike against the illegal and unhustified decision of the governing body.

He met secretary of the governing body and tried his best to convince him that the appointment of a school teacher as principal of the college is a matter of sub ordination and requested him to withdraw that decision.

The under matriculate secretary fumed and said;

You are an employee of our institution. I am a politician and sarpanch of the Grampanchayat where the college is located. You are staying in our local town. Do you think you know more about education than me? Go and teach English to the students. Don't interfere in our decision. The retired teacher Rasika Vatnagar is going to join on duty at the college in the next week. Our Odia lecturer Miss jhilki panda will welcome him garlanding at the threshold of his office room. She is living in a rented house adjacent to Rasika sir's building. Being a widower he very often takes help of our odia madam in his home work. She is very glad at our decision.

On the next day Manas held a staff meeting. He narrated how the secretary refused to change their decision. He also revealed the fact that odia madam Jhilki panda is supporting that retired teacher's appointment. When the staff wanted clarification from jhilki she said;

I am staying in his relative's house on rent. He is my next door neighbour. I have very good rapport with him. So I am not going to oppose him.

After half an hour of discussion Manas realised that maximum staff are afraid of opposing the governing body. They are ready to bow down before the unjust decision. The head clerk and the political science lecturer agreed with Manas and they decided to obstruct Rasik's entry into college.

Manas agreed with the head clerk Dukhiram Nath and assured him that he wouldn't not oppose . Both of them meet the pol.sc lecturer Ratnakar Gochhayat and communicated their decision to him. He agreed with them. They ate snacks , drank tea and returned to their homes.

The retired school teacher Rasika Vatnagar joined on duty on the next day. He maintained as usual works of the principal for a week. After a week he made a guideline that every employee of the college will come to his office at the time of arrival and departure. Every one has to salute him twice. No one can leave college without his permission. The basic objective of that guideline was to enforce landlordism and monopoly dominance on staff. After fifteen days he issued show cause notice to the employee who arrived at college 10 to 20 minutes late. Manas was expecting the staff to react but no one raised any objection. After a month Mr. Rasika held up salary of the staff to whom he had issued show cause notice. He said that he was not satisfied with the explanation of those employees.

It was a laughable matter. The salary of staff was a matter of shame to disclose in public. The lecturers were given 750 rupees , clerk and librarians 600 rupees and the peons 400 rupees per month. The amount was insufficient to meet expenses of tea and betel leaves. The staff whose salary was held up went to the principal's room to express their displeasure for such repressive step. He laughed and said;

Why are you worried? I will pay your salary. You take it now but you have be my followers. I and the governing body want to harass Manas and his friends who insulted me on my first day in this college. I hardly treat my adversaries as friends. Forgiveness is out of my dictionary. I am going to take

retaliatory action against Dukhiram, Ratnakar and Manas. You bring other staff to my residence at Malatipur town. I have nothing grudge against them. I want your cooperation to teach a lesson to Manas and his friends. They are underestimating me as a primary school teacher.

They oughtn't forget that the governing body is in my clutch.

I know that Manas is your staff association secretary. He has his own building in Malatipur town. He has good relation with the district and state level association of lectures and employees. He is very talented and courageous to challenge us but without staff cooperation he can't do so.

The librarian, P.E.T, Odia madam Jhilki and peon Sunguda took the charge of creating a split in staff association. Accordingly the lect. In Economics, Sociology, commerce joined hands with Jhilki and her group. They held a meeting with secretary of governing body at the residence of Rasika Vatnagar on a sunday afternoon and took decision to take repressive action against Dukhiram,Ratnakar and Manas. One of a governing body member informed Manas about that meeting and requested him not disclose his name.

Listening everything from Manas his wife Shilpa said;

You ought to intimate the matter to your followers. The governing body might take action against them. As I know they will not dare to take action against you.

Manas had strong faith on God and my ability to fight against injustice. He shared everything with Dukhiram and Ratnakar. All of them agreed to challenge the governing body if any repressive step is taken against any one of them.

CHAPTER 4

The secretary of governing body and the in-charge principal Rasika Vatnagar issued show cause notice to Dukhiram, Ratnakar and Manas concocting false and baseless allegations against them. They alleged that Ratnakar and Dukhiram had misappropriated college fund and shown obscene sign to the only lady teacher Miss Jhilki Panda. In the same way they brought allegation of neglect of duty, disobedience of authority and misdemeanour against Manas. They formed a jury consisting of two illiterate G.B. members, the secretary and Rasik Vatnagar. Manas, Ratnakar and Dukhiram were told to be present before the jury and to explain why disciplinary action wouldn't be taken against them within 15 days of getting the charge sheet against them. Ratnakar and Dukhiram discussed the matter with Manas. He said;

Mr. Rashika prabar Vatnagar is well known among the primary school teachers as mischief monger R. P. Vatnagar. Yesterday i met with one oh his colleague at Godaripatna primary school. He told me that in that he had adulterous relation with a lady teacher and mother of six children. He had been suspended twice for neglect of duty and stealing pulses meant for mid day meal of students. Once the village committee brought an opera party to stage drama during Christmas holidays at primary school field. Mr. R.P. Vatnagar told the village committee to give him percentage from profit. The members of village committee gave him through dressing with kicks, slaps and thrashing with sinew. He ran away from school field to save life. When the school reopened after holidays the villagers came to know that he had voluntarily transferred him to another school

. He is a sniper and coward. Thrashing is the only effective medicine for him. Here he would take help of our selfish staff members to retaliate on us. Don't be afraid. We will win over injustice.

Ratnakar and Dukhiram became happy. After college hour they returned to home.On the next day Manas remained absent from college on leave as he had some urgent domestic work. When Ratnakar and Dukhiramarrived at college Mr. R.P called them to his office and said;

Why did you try to outrage modesty of the only lady teacher when she was coming out from urinal. She shouted for help and the peon Sunguda arrived at the spot. It happened yesterday after my departure. Even most of the staff including your bosom friend Manas had gone out of college. The only lady teacher was late as she had gone to urinal. The peon Sunguda was locking rooms.

Ratnakar and Dukhiram got amazed to listen such lies. They said to Mr. R.P. Vatnagar;

Don't bring such allegation against our character. We are father of children. The lady teacher Jhilki has been working with us for last 10 years. Call him to your office. We want to ask her the reason behind telling such lies.

Miss Jhilki panda was overhearing everything standing behind door curtain of the principal's door. She rushed inside like a tornado and Mr. R.P. went out of his room. She closed door of the principal's room, torn her blouse and embraced Ratnakar from his back. She shouted in a loud voice;

Save me, Save me, They are outraging my modesty forcibly. Dukhiram opened the door and asked Ratnakar to run away. Mr. R.P. shouted in a loud voice;

They have raped the only lady teacher. Chase after them.

The peon sunguda, lady teacher jhilki and their group started running after Ratnakar and Dukhiram. The other people joined with them and shouted;

Catch, Catch the rapist is sneaking. Hundreds of people started running on the road as if a marathon was taking place. Nobody thought it proper to know the truth.

They hid themselvesf inside the office room of Ratnakar's friend who was watch man of R. I. Office of that panchayat. The people couldn't catch them.

The secretary of the college, a few G.B. members arrived at college with police van and a few reportrers of local odia news paper. They recorded lady teacher Jhilki's statement in presence of hundreds of local people and the goers of that adjoining road. Showing her torn blouse and bra she said;

The lewd political science lecturer Ratnakar had sinful eyes on her blonde maiden body. She had felt that many times from his leer. The headclerk Dukhiram appealed her for sex before two years in a state of inebriation. She had slapped on his face. On that day he begged forgiveness holding my two legs and i forgave him.

Ratnakar and Dukhiram followed me when I came out of urinal. They entered into the principal's room behind me. When I signing on attendance register Ratnakar embraced me tightly from back and kneaded my nipples. Dukhiram entered his middle and index finger into my vulva and unbuttoned my blouse. When I resisted he pulled my blouse with bra . Ratnakar wanted to make me fall on the ground but I came out of room kicking at his sensitive organ.

The police recorded statement of witnesses. The peon Sunguda, the librarian and sociology lecturer gave their statement. The reporters took photograsphs of Miss. Jhilkiin in different angles and promised to make the matter their front page news. The in-charge principal held two different meeting s with the police and the reporters. It was open secret that he gave money to them for making the case strong and viral.

The reporters took an interview of Miss Jhilki as she has done something very valourous by protecting her from the gang rapists. Miss Jhilki alleged that Dukhiram and Ratnakar are very salacious and corrupted. They would n't spare the girl students to fecundate if such chance comes to their hand. The reporters giggled and said;

Mr. R.P. Vatnagar is very an ardent philogynist. He will definitely take hard step against the lecherous men and caddish fellows. Miss Jhilki shook hands of the reporters and gave adieu to them.

The police registered a case of molestation and attempt to murder against Ratnakar and Dukhiram. The governing body dismissed them from service. They absconded to avoid arrest and applied for advance bail in the High court. Manas met with them when they were living in the house of Dukhiram's relative out of district. He expressed regret over the ugly things happened in college and assured them of acquittal from concocted case.

They got bail from high court. Manas helped them to raise voice against unjustified dismissal order of G.B. in a press conference. In that press conference they declared that they would appeal against the dismissal at Employees Tribunal and in the court of the Director of Higher Education. The governing body became angry with Manas who condemned low profile of the G. B. Members and defects in Govt. provision for opening of private college and functions of G. B. He found the whole system defective and antithetical to the nature , scope and norms of education.

The governing body issued Manas's dismissal order and sent the letter by registered post to his house address. He was not surprised to receive the letter as the secretary and Mr. R.P. Vatnagar had threatened him not to go against them. He gladly accepted the letter and decided to put forth their grievances before the Commissioner- cum-Secretary to Govt. in Higher Education.

The District Association of Lecturers and Employees wanted them to launch a strike demanding dismissal of a retired teacher from post of principal of a recognised and affiliated college. Manas agreed and gave prior report about their hunger strike tothe District Administrartion. Hundreds of lecturers and employees of different colleges congregated in front of Manas's college and sat inside the tent meant for Hunger Strike. The police van, water tank, medical van and reporters arrived at the hunger strike spot. All participants took vow touching portraits Gandhi that they would not call off the strike till notorious retired old school teacher is not dismissed from the post of in-charge principal. Everybody gave slogan against Mr. R.P. Vatnagar's illegal appointment, against false rape case framed by G.B. with help of Miss. Jhilki and illegal dismissal of senior employees from service. As secretary of the Staff Association of his college Manas gave introductory speech briefing about all anti institutional, arbitrary, illegal and repressive works of the illegal principal in- charge and G.B. There after the State President, the Secretary of District Association gave speech and condemned functions of G.B. They pointed out the defects in Govt. rules and regulations for formation of G.B. The lay man members of G.B. are given power to govern fate of the post graduate lecturers. It is ludicrous and highly condemnable.

The ex- Secretary of the college and the then Secretary arrived at the spot of hunger strike along with a few G. B. Members and gave a proposal that they would revoke dismissal order of staffand remove Mr. R.P. Vatnagar from job at college. They took a week's time and an agreement was made between the Staff Association and G.B. A few witnesses also signed on the agreement paper along with Secretataries of G.B. and Staff Association.

The president of State Association of lecturers read out the agreement paper and asked Manas to call off the hunger strike.

Manas gave his speech of thanks to all and highly eulogised the District Association and District Administration for their kind support for the noble cause of up keeping holistic abode of an educational institution. He declared that the strike was put off.

The hunger strike came to an end in an atmosphere of joy, faith, trust and good wishes. Manas emerged as the victorious leader of his team. Everybody praised him and he expressed gratitude.

CHAPTER 5

Being dismissed from service as lect. In English Manas lost faith on education, knowledge, skill, good character and sincere attempt to do something good for others.He became very unhappy over soulless education without merit and proficiency. He closed coaching centre and joined in real estate business. He had a home loan on his head. One of his well wisher helped him in real estate business. He had been working as a broker in sale and purchase of land for last ten years. He was earning 50 thousand to 1 lakh rupees brokerage for a successful land deal.

Manas started working with him and became familiar with all land brokers of Malatipur town. Manas had proficiency of settling any deal between two parties. So he became master in the new trade within a few months of his entry to real estate business. Mr. V. K. Biswas was a reputed land plotter of Malatipur. Being dismissed from his bank service he had started land plotting before 5 years and became a man of multi crores. Manas joined hands with him. Within two months Manas and his partner made two sale deeds and got above one lakh commission. They took 50 thousand each and kept 10 thousand as joint fund for fuel, snacks and meal expenses till the next land deal. Day to day Manas became a prominent name for the real estate brokers and plotters. A group of brokers became his business associates and friends.

He gave 50 thousand rupees to his wife Shilpa. She became very happy as the family was in bare need of money to pay electric bill, to book gas cylinder, to clear credit of the grocer, to pay dues of their youngest son who was reading in a convent school and many such heads of unavoidable expenses.

In the afternoon they visited some plots and talked with the land owners about rate and their commission. He returned to home at 8 P.M. keeping the bike inside the drawing room he went to bed room and slept. His wife Shilpa helped him to put off paint and shirt. He slept till 8A.M .i the next morning. He found 5to 6 unattended calls from Kailas on his cellphone and hurriedly completed routine work, He put on paint and new baniyan and went out of home. At that time Shilpa was worshipping in God's room. Seeing Manas going out of home she came out and said;

Wait, I am going to make tea for you. You drunk yesterday and didn't take supper. At least take some snacks.

Manas said;

I have taken 1000 rupees from almirah. We have to show plots to 5 to 6 buyers. It seems that a new deal may be finalised. We will have our snacks and lunch outside. I will take bath at the road side Dhaba . I have kept napkin inside dickie. We are going to Agarpada to meet with a buyer and finalise the matter for registration of the plot which that buyer has selected. He wants us at his home to finalise rate and to give advance for sale deed. Pray God for success of the deal. We have to pay 3 months instalment amount of the housing loan, LIC renewal premium and admission fees of both sons.

Manas started his bike and met with Kailas at his betel shop. He had been waiting for him for 2 hours. So he closed the shop and told Manas to drive to the liquor off shop at kuansha of Malatipur town. Manas couldn't understand as they had tour programme to the buyer's house at Agarpada. Kailas said;

We drunk 6 beers yesterday. Due to over drink he feels laziness. One or two pegs of alcohol is necessary to get relief from hang over. We will have our snacks at the stall near liquor counter.

Manas parked his bike beside the liquor shop. Kailas took 300 rupees from him and wanted his suggestion about the premium brand of whisky he was going to purchase. Manas suggested him to buy Blenders Pride whisky.

Kailas prepared 2 pegs mixing with cold drink. At first Manas refused to drink but again he thought about his loss of job at college and inner frustration after serving in college for 14 years without grant-in-aid and approval of post. He held the glass for a few minutes and quaffed. Kailas laughed and said;

Remove all thoughts of your college job and be happy that no one can snatch your knowledge. Take another peg and be happy that we are going to earn1.5 lakhs from this deal with Agarpada buyer.

They arrived at the buyer Alok Sutar's house. He requested them to finalise the rate of 35 thousand per decimal. He was going to purchase 15 decimil for opening of a garage. Manas and kailash had told him to pay 40 thousand per decimal. The land ownner's rate was 25 thousand per decimal. So they agreed and made a condition that the buyer would give 20 thousand to them as tips.

The buyer agreed and that deal was finalised. He gave 20 thousand in advance and got ready for sale deed in the next week.

They came out of Mr. Sutar's house and stood near a betel shop. Manas wanted to go to a road side Dhaba for bath and lunch but Kailash wanted to go to a liquor off shop. He said;

We are getting 10 thousand each. You needn't spend. I am going to spend from my share of 10 thousand rupees. Your partnership with me is going to be very lucky for me. I am an illiterate man. The deal became possible because of your presence. Your higher qualification and to the point talks impressed him. Let us drink another whisky of 180ml. Of the same brand. Having drunk we will visit the Dhaba and have our lunch.

Manas smiled and appreciated Kailash's home spun knowledge of practicality of life. He took kailash to the nearest liquor off shop. They purchased a Blenders Pride whisky bottle of 360ml. They ate boiled egg and fish fry as snacks with liquor.They emptied half bottle and left the liquor shop. Manas drove his bike very cautiously and reached at Kalika Dhaba. They ordered for bread and mutton. While they were eating another land broker named Rasananda arrived at the Dhaba. Kailas invited him to share drinking. Again he paid 500 rupees to the sales man to fetch a Blenders Pride whisky of 180 ml. They spent the whole 2 hours at the Dhaba and returned to Malatipur.

Manas arrived at home. His wife became very unhappy to see that he had drunk. Manas changed his dress and went into the bath room. After bath he put on clean cloth and entered into God's room for evening prayer. He prayered God for health and happiness of his family.

While sipping tea he said to Shilpa;

By blessings of God that land deal became successful. We are going to get 1.5 lakhs commission. The buyer had given 20 thousand advance. My share of 10 thousand is in my pocket. Kailas spent the whole amount except 300 hundred for fuel from common fund of previous deal. We have drunk much. You should forgive me for drinking every day. I may earn lakhs but it is very painful to a new identity of a land broker. I have inarticulate agonies. Let me enjoy a new phase of wanton pleasure and agog of huge commission.

Tears rolled down the cheeks of Shilpa. She requested him to sleep and prayed God for safety and wellness of her family.

CHAPTER 6

Once Manas was enjoying drinks at a bar of Malatipur town. One of his companion a land broker Nahia told him that a number of poor unmarried girls were attending hotels of the town as call girls. They were coming to the hotel by agents who give customers for their bodies and take commission. The sex racket was running in full swing in Zebra Cross hotel and lodge. The agents of sex racket flocked at the vestibule of lord Shiva temple at the back side of lodge.Their business hour was from 3 P.M TO 8 P.M. Manas knew that Nahia was a tall talker.He didn't believe in his words. So he said to Nahia;

How is it possible? Malatipur is a small town. There are 4 to 5 hotel-cum-lodge. In the day time many customers visit the restaurants of the hotel. You might have seen girls going in or coming out from the restaurants.

Nahia said;

The poor girls are coming for prostitution by their reliable agents. Many of them are reading in colleges. They belong to the adjoining villages of Malatipur Block. They return back home before 9 P.M. Nobody can doubt them as they pretend of visiting Malatipur town for coaching, shopping or for medical check up whatever come to their mouths. If you stand on the left side of Zebra Cross hotel you will see all activities taking place. you will find girls coming out from the hotel one after another at intervals covering their face with stoles.

Manas thought for a while and decided to check Nahia's report about girls and sex racket. He came out of bar with Nahia at 6 P. M. Nahia went to his home but Manas to the side that hotel. He parked his bike and stood silently. 20

minutes passed he found nothing happening as to Nahia's report of sex business. He was about to start his bike suddenly his eyes fell on two girls who came out of the hotel and hurriedly sneaked from sight. Manas heard starting sound of a four wheeler parked on the road side about 300 metres away from the hotel. As he left to the left side of the hotel he saw girls going in and coming out from the hotel at successive intervals by the back side door. A few men were waiting at lord Shiva temple. They were the agents who were making all arrangements for quick departure of girls after sex with paid customers.

It was going to be 8 P. M. The vestibule Shiva temple became deserted. Manas was sitting alone and thinking about lives even the fast changing pace of lives even at the small towns. His fell on a girl standing alone near back door of the hotel. He went near the girl and asked;

Why are you standing? Where is your agent? It seems the agent has forgotten to take you back to your house.

The girl cried and said;

I am a poor girl. My parents are in sick bed. I have a tailoring shop at Padmapur market. Please drop me at my home. I will give fuel cost to you.

Manas became angry and said to her;

Why shall I help you? You are selling your body to others. I have no money but I can make you arrested by reporting the matter to the police. You can't show your face to anybody.

She sobbed and said;

I have no objection. You enjoy my body if you have safe room. I must return home before 10 P.M.

Manas started his bike and allowed her to sit. He had no extra room or friends to whom he could rely on. So he took the girl on main road to her home. On the way there was a convent school. He thought of taking her to the back side that convent school building for sex with her. She understood his intention and agreed. Parking the bike on road side both of them started walking to the backside of that building. The school watchman shouted at them to stop. Manas said;

She wants to attend call of nature. Please allow her to use lavatory.

The watchman allowed her. She came out of lavatory after 5minutes. Manas started his bike and she sat at his back. He was looking for a suitable place to enjoy that girl all along his way. He saw a burial ground and tank on the road side. The girl's village Padmapur was only 2 kilometres away. He parked his bike and kissed her. She said;

Go there and enjoy me on the bank of this tank.

Before he could answer she laughed and said;

It is your bad luck. Look the people are coming to cremate a dead body.

As the funeral procession came near Manas came to know that an unmarried girl of the nearby fisherman clan was caught red handed having adulterous relation with a married man. She hanged herself to save her face.

Manas took a long breath and said to the girl with him;

Don't spoil yourself like the girl going to be burnt at the burial ground.

That girl nodded her head. He drove his bike and arrived at the girl's village.He dropped her on the main road of the village and watched her walking briskly on a lane to her house.On his way back to home he thanked God for not giving him the chance to have sex with that girl.

CHAPTER 7

Manasa's income from land land brokerage increased from day to day. It helped him fulfil all requirements of a middle class family. He spent the whole day roaming with land brokers to show plots to the buyers and to collect land records from the sellers. More than 30 land brokers got associated with him. Most of them were habitual drunkards. Whenever they started journey to any area for a business deal they definitely stopped near the liquor shop on the way to drink and to decide the future course of action. Sometimes the rehearsal for land deals were held near the liquor counters. So he became familiar with all liquor counters and bars of Malatipur town and its adjoining block areas. Every day he met with many known faces at different liquor counters and developed a kind of kinship. A few of them advised him not to drink but maximum encouraged him to enjoy life. He preferred silence to maintain good relation with everybody and to avoid unnecessary bickering in state of inebriation.

He never shared the matters relating to job as lecturer except telling them that there was a conflict with staff and governing body and as a result a few staff like him were not attending the college. They had gone to the court for justice. Most of the land brokers were illiterate or under matriculate. So they had nothing idea about governing body and grant-in- aid policy of Govt. But all of them had faith on court. They assured him of getting all benefits of job by court order.

He became a habitual drunkard within a year of regular drinking with his real estate associates. The sales man of many liquor counters became his close friends. Every day he spent a few hours near the liquor counter for drinking and eating snacks at the nearby stalls. Sometimes he bought liquor bottles on credit and paid the amount in his next visit to that liquor counter.

He drank liquor like water and drove his bike like a normal man without addiction. His associates were very often surprised to find that he was not abnormal even after sufficient intake of alcohol. They happily certified him a big drunkard. A few of them also complimented him for normal politeness even in a state of addiction. As time rolled on his land deals increased. He celebrated each successful deal with his associates in drinking and feasting.

One day Manas and his three land dealing associates stared drinking liquor at 10 A.M in the morning at a sub rural area of Malatipur town. They had executed a big land deal before two days. He had got a lion' share of the total brokerage amount and his associates had got 1 lakh each. He was king pin of that deal and his other associates just helped him in measurement of the plot doing sundry works like pulling chain and digging holes for cement pillars. Out of sympathy and friendship, Manas had given one lakh to each of them. They looked upon him as their leader and they had total faith on his justice to the team. They were ignorant of the total commission obtained from that land deal. As they got one lakh each they became very happy as it was beyond their expectation. So, they also wanted to celebrate the successful land deal drinking liquor up to the throat. They took a cabin at Thomasim Dhaba just 100 meters away from a big liquor shop close to NH 5. A raw of castor plants had made a canopy at North side of the liquor shop. It was month of April. The cattle were roaming in the open field close to the counter. Manas and his associates went on taking snacks like boiled egg, chicken pakoda and fried bin as snacks of a pegs of whisky. They emptied two bottles of 360 ml whisky before lunch. After taking lunch with dishes of mutton curry and hot rice, they again enjoyed drinking seating near the castor plant, they spewed six pieces of old news paper on the floor as mat. They could not know how time passed and evening arrived. They had slept in a state of inebriation. The liquor shop owner made them awake at 7 PM. Manas searched for his mobile, money purse and key of the bike, he became very unhappy to find everything missing. The shop keeper smiled and said I have kept your purse, mobile and key. All of you had lost your sense. Many people came drank and went away. Three of you spent the whole day in my counter, out of sympathy, I took care of your

inebriated state. I would like to request you for avoiding such boozing. You may die from excess consumption of alcohol.

Manas listened to good advice of the liquor shop owner and laughed. The shop keeper was surprised. I know that you are a highly educated man as I had your oratory English with my sells men. Manas stopped laughing and thanked the liquor shop owner for his humanity, he said to him to do something for others is humanity and to do something for the self is just a substance of living. When we feel pain we are alive, when we feel pain of others, we are alive in higher level of consciousness. Life and death are not the matter to be taken care of your ignore, but the conscience indicates and social sense pervades to have precaution and preparation for better living. I laughed as I realised that much of the things happened to life without our expectation and despite precaution to avoid. The liquor shop owner thanked him and said I have great regard for the sensible man like you. As I overheard from the discussion among yourselves I came to know that you have some trouble with your job and as a result you are roaming with land brokers.

Manas smiled and said to him my companion Kailash might have given you my identity at present I am in a land broker's role. We have nothing identity like that of water having no shape. It takes shape as to the container in the likely way. Life invites us to different fields as to the role assigned or the role adopted.

Again he thanked the liquor shop owner while receiving his mobile, purse and keys from his counter. He started his bike and asked his companions to share seat on his bike and to start their bike also. It was difficult to keep balance but Manas said to himself " we have spent many hours seating idle and sleeping. The body has got sufficient rest. It is a question of mental nervousness or some impact of intoxication that was blocking normal balance. He stopped the start and drink sufficient cold water before leaving the place and touching NH 5 on his bike.

CHAPTER 8

Leaving home after routine works of the day by 8A.M, roaming outside in connection with land deal, eating at hotel and drinking liquor with land dealers became a new habit with Manas. A towel, one soap and empty once use glasses were always kept inside the dickey of his bike. In the summer season very often he took bath at roadside Dhaba. While taking bath at Dhaba he followed the truck drivers style of taking two to three pegs just after bath before taking lunch. The same pace of life continued for 2 years. His college colleagues were barely in need of Manas's company for reinstatement in job. Manas told them to wait for another six months as he had two more big land deals. He was sure to get more than 1.5 lakhs from those two land deals. It was the month of February, Manas and his six associates went to Maidapur to finalise a land deal with a real estate company named Delta Real estate and Housing. The M. D. of that company had a project for fishing. He wanted to buy 30 acres of land at a spot. One land broker of Markona, two land brokers of Maidapur and three land brokers of Ranital were given the charge to collect land in the middle of Maidapur and Markona. They collected 22 acres of land belonging to six big farmers with assurance that their wards would be given job opportunity in that hatchery project. A team of seven members was formed to finalise the deal with Manas as the leader. Accordingly he met with M.D of that company and said,

Sir, It is a difficult and complex task to collect 30 acres land near Ranital and Maidapur as all lands are high yielding irrigated agricultural plots. You ought to make an agreement with us for the task and give advance of at least

1 lakh rupees. After such agreement, we will hand over you land records of 22 acres. Within a fortnight the 8 acres of land record will be collected from the buyers. Everyday my people are working hard to give shape to the project. They have tour expenses along with snacks and tea expenses for the land owners. Sometimes they have to entertain to land owner with drinks, chicken or mutton as the land owners also face problems to convince their family members for selling the high yielding lands to a Company. Collecting 30 acres of land at a place is not a easy task at all. Even after collecting records of land for sale again the same sellers withdraw telling their problems with the family members, so, you made the agreement with us and gave a cash or cheque of one lank within one month the sale deed will be finalised. The MD agreed to his words and called for an Advocate to prepare an agreement between the

Marketing Manager and Manas for sale deed. Having signed the agreement and got the cheque, Manas started his bike from Balasore and arrived at Maidapur by 3 PM. They encash the cheque at Markona Bank where the Company had an Account. Every members of his team became very happy. All of them went to side Dhaba at Maidapur for further discussion, drink and snacks. He gave 10 thousand to each of his land associates and kept 40 thousand in his hand towards Encumbrance Certificate and supervision of overall preparation for the sale deed as to the agreement of the Court papers. His land dealing associates went on calculating how much brokerage would come from sale deed of 30 acres of land. If they get one lakh for each acres then it would be 30 lakhs. Manas laughed and said do not count the chickens before they are hatched. The sales manager of the Company would take 50% of the brokerage as he is not one, they have a group of marketing managers for Balasore district. They have convinced the MD of the Company for which he agreed to my words and gave an advance of 1 lakh rupee. The agreement has been made between me and the Marketing Manager of the Company. We may defy but the Marketing Manager would be responsible for 1 lakh rupee as the Company would recollect the amount from his salary if the sale deed would fail. One of his business associate begged forgiveness and said we have no such qualification like you, if we get 50 thousand each it would be a great help for our family. For every day expenses till the sale deed, we each can expense 10 thousand. Whenever you come to supervise, the collection of land records, you have to provide bottle and snacks to us. Manas laughed and agreed to their conditions. He said the amount might not be the exact but you are going to get one lakh each from such a big deal.

As he had 10 thousand in his pocket, his business associates wanted to enjoyed drinking up to their throat. From 5 PM to 9 PM, they sat in the Dhaba eating chicken pokada and drinking whisky. After 8 PM, Manas and other two brokers of Maidapur lost their sense. The Dhaba owner and his sales man sprinkled water on their face and gave tamarind water to drink. At about 10.30 PM, Manas became normal. His friends escorted him up to his house at Malatipur town, driving his bike and carrying him in the middle. That day his family members could not help crying seeing his condition. His wife and wards wanted him to leave land brokerage and to fight for re-instatement of his job at College. Manas listened to their words and cried because he could not utter words due to severe pain in his chest. His family members nursed him up to 2 PM. After that he slept in deep sleep and got up from bed at 9 AM in the morning. Having taken his birth, he came to the Gods' house and found his wife Shilpa worshiping the deities. She gazed his face and said in a stammering voice " God saved your life, you had come to the house in a half dying state. We all are depended on you. There is no other one to take care of me and our children. How dare to die without killing all of us. If you feel that you have no zest for life, love for us and no care for earthly joy and purpose, you tell us frankly, I will purchase a poison bottle from the market and all of us will take poison together.

Now her voice chocked. She trembled like a palm leaf and started beating her head on the floor. Manas held her head by his two hands and cried out in shrilling voice, his whole body got desuderated. In the mean while, his youngest son came to the Room like a befooled passenger in a tyre busted in deluxe coach high speedy bus. Manas eyes fell on English edition of Srimad Bhabat Gita kept on the self of God's rooma. The picture of lod Krishna charioting Arjun for the battle of Kurukhetra, stroke his mind like an arrow. He

said to his wife, the archer Arjuna was not prepared to fight Kurukhetra for property. Lord Krishna explained him that he had nothing to fear for as He was with him, but Lord Arjun could not believe in Krishna's power and apprehended great lost to Pandavas as there were great warriors like Drona and Karna and thousands of well armed soldiers. On the side of Kaurava's he thought that they five brothers and Lord Krishna were too weak to face them. Lord Krishna laughed and showed his expended version of the world. Now Arjun bowed down before his feet and lifted his bow and arrows . In the likely way, When the Europeans in their old testament told that the earth was like a plate, if somebody goes to the border he might fell down were ignorant of Indian theology. Thousands years before in Vishnu Purana, when lord Krishna had taken the incarnation of Baraha had lifted the round earth from the sea and in the child hood, lord Krishna had shown to his mother the round earth with all planets and constellation of starts in his mouth. It proved that the Indians scriptures were repleted with the intrinsic facts of creation of the earth. The scientific accuracy of facts in Indian theology is a matter of research for the whole world.

His wife thought that Manas was telling all these things as he was not free from alcoholic intoxication. Manas set down by her side and asked his son to seat on the floor. He said I am telling all these things to make you know that the things are allowed to happen with a good cause in it. I was drinking everyday and taking it as a panacea for remedy of all problems. As I fainted and came to a half dying state, you as well as my land dealing associates got

afraid and advised me not to drink. Today, I took promise seating at the God's room in front of my divine mentors that I am parting with liquor at this moment for good. Life as a matter of Karma, Dharma, Destiny and harvest from the previous birth are always the matters to be reckoned with. The kernels of knowledge enshrined in Shrimad Bhagavad Geeta , Upanished and Vedas are matters of scientific research for the whole world.

At this moment I feel that what happened was the unpleasant past with a greater cause to pave for the pleasant present.

CHAPTER 9

The Govt. of Odisha in the Dept. Of Higher education has already issued letter to The Regional Director of Education, Bhubaneswar for a spot visit to Manas's college and to authenticate the staff position. Manas and his colleagues arrived at the office of R. D.E at about 3P.M. They gave written slips of their names to meet the RDE in chair. Being permitted Manas, Ratnakar and Dukhiram meet him and narrated all illegal and repressive steps of the governing body that looks upon college their personal business centre. They were taking all money from students collection for their personal expenses. They hardly paid salary to the staff. They treated the lecturers as their hired labourers. No one was allowed to open mouth against their anti institutional and monopoly exploitation of staff. That why the G.B. appointed a retired teacher as principal in charge and took vindictive step against the out spoken senior staff of the college framing concocted charges.

The RDE took pity on them and assured of his visit to the college in the next week. Coming out of his office they went to the canteen inside that office campus. While they were discussing sorrowful matters relating to their job , monopoly retaliatory activities of the G.B two staff of RDE were sipping tea. One of them was found very attentive to their discussion. He was listening and observing their body language.Having sipped tea he talked with them and wanted to know their present state of living condition. Manas discussed all matters in deatail s to him. He assured them of all possible help. Manas realised that a bond of friendship was cgoing to be cemented. So he collected contact number of that staff named Jeevan Das, the dealing assistant of RDE.

Jeevan Das, the dealing assistant was a man of good heart. He was living with his wife and daughter in rented house very close to his father-in-law's house. His wife was a teacher. In his next visit to RDE he spent a night at Jeevan's house. Both of them spent many hours at night discussing personal affairs, problems of staff in private colleges and matters relating to politics and government.He took the charge of convincing RDE for taking necessary steps to save the staff of the college from mental torture, social degradation and financial paucity. On the next day he requested the staff in charge of RDE'S tour management to fix an early date of visit to Manas's college.

Coming from Bhubaneswar Manas communicated the matter to his colleagues. They became happy and expected something very positive from the RDE's spot inquiry and authentication. After five days the RDE arrived at the college.He scrutinised all records of the college, verified staff attendance, G.B. resolution book, staff acquittance registerand talked with all staff.

He didn't allow the secretary or any governing body member to be inside the college premises. After verification of records and conversation with all staff the RDE returned to Bhubaneswar. Every staff anticipated right authentication of staff position by him. On next day Manas telephoned to Jeevan and became happy to know that the staff authentication letter was going to be released in the evening. The letter being released in the RDE website Jeevan communicated the letter no to Manas. The letter was addressed to the Director Higher Education with memo to the sub collector-cum- Special Officer of the college. He down loaded the letter from a cybercafé and thanked the almighty for justice to the aggrieved and harassed employees like he and his friends.

CHAPTER 10

The inquiry report of the RDE and staff authentication letter reached the office of Additional Secretary to Govt. in the Dept. of Higher Education with recommendation for reinstatement of the suspended/ dismissed employees in service without break of service period.Manas visited the secretariate with one of his friend to monitor advancement of their college file. He met with the Additional Secretary to Govt. and the Commissioner-cum- secretary to Govt. in the Dept. of higher Education five to six times within two months. Finally the govt. order for reinstatement without break of service period came out on an auspicious day of November 2012. His seven years of persistent struggle to get justice finally ended with success.

Manas and his friends resumed their works in the college. The sub collector-cum-special officer counter signed claimant details of the staff and trans mitted to Director Higher education for release of Grant-in=aid as per GIA Order 2OO8. Finally the college was notified as an aided educational institution and service of all staff was approved by Govt. It was victory of order and justice over disorder and anarchy.

Those years of struggle was a big lesson for life. He became aware of all callous and insensible system of service at private colleges in the hands of amateur governing body. He and his colleagues got freedom from many years of exploitation and harassment. Their family members also felt a shower of rain after many years of man made drought and famine. The day on which they received salary from Govt. was the day of bright sun shine after many years of cloudy sky.

As per his vows before God and Goddess for success Manas and his family members visited Goddess Shyamakali at Laxmannath king's palace and Lord Chandaneswar Mahadev. They offered prayer and worship. They offered 108 coconuts to Goddess Tarini at Ghatagaon and sent their eldest son to bring ambrosia of Lord Jagannath, puri. In this way Manas and his wife spent a whole month visiting temples and offering worship and oblation.

His pace of life became smooth, certain and dignified. He had long dream of recording his emotion, experiences and lessons from life in literature. Like a squirrel on banana buoy he had encountered many floods and flush floods in life for safe arrival at shore. I was God's mercy on him that he had narrowly escaped from death many times when he was boozing day and night. In his child hood he had heard from his mother that God's desire his final and binding. The course of life is controlled by His direction and will. Those who extend their cooperation in the struggling days of life are the messengers of God. Life is a big university of practical learning. It bristles with challenges and possibilities. There is nothing to despond. Life's dessert lies in devotion to destination.

CHAPTER 11

As a novelist and story teller he was a like a squirrel on banana buoy in the flood of dishonesty and defilement of sanctity of all constitutional bodies for recognition of talent and proper justice. Political nepotism and despotism, vested interest, cheap advertisement, corruption has devoured all institutions for proper evaluation of the writers' talent. He had nothing to despond. All his endeavour to evaluate ups and downs of life seemed to him a worthless analysis.

Why he will be unhappy for the things which are not in his hands.The gargantuan corrupted society is selfish and callous to every new comer in the field. The conflict between devotion to destination and obstacles is not new for any society and for any profession. He wanted to push back such conflict lurking from experiences of life but its grip was too strong to push back without an analysis of what was, what is and what might be.

His wife was ill with severe cold and fever. Day to day she was getting ailing and spiritless to do any work with normal mirth and vigour. Her obesity was a main problem for her locomotive. She felt mild joint pain and exasperation while walking. Looking at his wife's faded swelling face and corpulent body he asked to himself;

Was she the right dream damsel of his youth? His heart replied in negative. Then he asked if she was not the right choice how he fell in love with her. The echoes of heart became feeble but it whispered that love originated from wild irresistible biological instinct to test the joy of touching fair organs of woman. In those days he was almost a frantic to behold beauty of woman. His strong beastial passion found curiosity in Shilpa's big nipples and buttock.

He got thrilled to play with her disrobed body. That game of sex went for months together. He felt himself guilty of desecrating her maidenhood and accepted her as his better half.

In his puberty he had dreamed for a slim blonde with lustrous eyes, dimple cheeks, light feet and apple blossom. His dream damsel had bewitching beauty and enticing glamour. She was like a murmuring cascade of a siren.

Shilpa had neither bewitching beauty nor feminine gesture to captivate any man.She was a half educated countryside girl of moderate beauty and docile nature. She hardly take care of embellishment of her body. She had no craze for gaudy dress, aroma, cosmetics, ornaments and luxurious way of up to date life. She was complacent with her lot and thankful to God for providing her all happiness which she had never dreamed of, desired for or schemed with a mesh.

He diverted his mind from thoughts about his love affair and marriage and liked to analyse his professional choice of place of work and colleagues. When he asked the question to himself whether he wanted to be a lecturer at the very outset of his master degree in English literature, Whether he enjoyed his job as lecturer in English, Whether his place of work was up to his expectation and satisfaction, Whether his colleagues were up to his expected standard for intellectual co sharing of day to day life and problems in the system of education, Whether terewas intimacy among them beyond the professional link he was not amazed to get all answers in negatives.

It was his mother's dream to make him a doctor or magistrate. Her first option was to see him a doctor.That is why being amiddle class widow she took the financial burden of his admission in science stream at Bhadrak college which was 140 kilomtres distance from his native place. He couldn't fulfil her mother's dream because of his early craze for sex. He got entagled in the sex trap of a mother and her daughter.

He started working as a lecturer in private college when he had earned name and fame as a resourceful tacher in English in his coaching. His mother persuaded him to give examination for the post of administrator even after his joining in the private college. He couldn't fulfil her second dream because of his family burden and capricious temperament for career.

Once he sat for OAS examination and qualified the preliminary. His rank was within 10 among the successful candidates though more than 50 thousand candidates had appeared in the preliminary examination. He prepared for OAS Main Examination in a selective way. He went through previous question papers of OAS examination for ten years and prepared answers to those questions in his optional papers. His selective way of preparation became very effective for him except International relation paper. The examination for that paper was his last optional paper. He had done very well in all other papers. In that paper he didn't find a single question as to his selection. He became very sad. He tried to answer the questions in the likely way of moving a stick in darkness to hit the target. He came out of the

examination hall after one hour of examination and broke the news to his wife Shilpa. His wife said;

What are doing now?

Manas said;

I am unable to answer any question correctly. Now I am out of the examination hall and talking with you from a telephone booth. I am going to hand over my answer script to the invigilator very soon. What shall I do sitting idle inside the hall for whole duration of the examination.

His wife said;

You do whatever you feel right to do.

Manas laughed and said;

I know that you can't suggest or persuade but you are always happy with what ever comes on the way.

His choice to be a lecturer in English came spontaneously as he enjoyed the joy of giving coaching in English and earned his lively hood before joining in the college. English was his favourite subject from child hood. He had inborn eloquence and mastery over teaching. The students and guardians highly appreciated his innovative way of teaching. He earned name and fame as resourceful teacher in English.

As to his choice of place of work he found himself a tomfool. Why did he join in a newly established college at a rural area? Why didn't he think about the illiterate rural environment and its distance from Mlatipur town?

All such analysis are worthless. It also happened to him. Oneday the clerk of that newly established college met him at Malatipur town and invited him to join in that college. They had collected information about his excellence as a teacher in English from the students and guardians of that locality. The clerk made it clear that the secretary was in search of an expert English hand.

Manas said;

I don't like to give donation for job in a private college.

The clerk said nothing but took him to have a direct communion with the Secretary who was at Kachery Bazar of Malatipur town for his personal work.

In that meeting it was decided that Manas would join in that college without donation and he would het 500 rupees as salary per month. He would have to spend 2to 3 hours in the college as to college time table.

He agreed and joined in that college as lecturer in English first post. Years rolled on. He coped with the colleagues but was never satisfied with them. There was no intellectual environment. The local men having requisite qualification had joined in that college. Most of them had average student career. They had no depth and resource in concerned subjects. Three and half decades passed with them. They always wanted him to be their leader for official works and functions but they failed to reciprocate to his talent. It happened perhaps for two reasons. They couldn't see themselves inferior or they took it granted that a prophet is not honoured in his own locality.

There might be a third reason and it is the chronic sentiment of the people of Odisha in general. Every body in Odisha thinks himself or herself the Know All. Everybody likes to talk a lot without listening to the best talks of others.The people of Odisha are perhaps emotional or selfish or spiteful to praise and recognise others talent.

Another amusing fact which he experienced as writer relates to the no. of writers in Odisha who are skirmishing literature market now a days. Whether they are writers or pseudo writers is never debated. The ignorance and credulity of Odisha people are really pitiable. Both the print media and electronics media in Odisha have become marketed commodities. So knowledge, ignorance, merit, demerit, truth , lie, honesty , dishonesty are not properly brought before the people.

While analysing the things of be gone days, the days at hand and expectation from the days ahead he became very thoughtful . He found no body to be blamed for the things that he couldn't achieve or nothing to despond as life is a living experience of many things that happen to it. All precaution and preparation are a part of journey of life but not the inevitable go of it. Very often the meticulous plan fail, the merit is bypassed, the culprit is acquitted, the daft is recognised and awarded, the charlatans are acknowledged as honest pedants and lie kick back truth to the corner. Nobody has time to ponder over. Let it go is the go now.

In this hostile conspiratorial world the analysis of life seems worthless. There is no option but to surrender to the lot. The only solace is the sincere endeavour in direct direction to realise the ways to live life to its full learning lessons from it to avoid worthless analysis of who I was.

CHAPTER 12

It was going to be 5P.M. So he got up from bed and took his pet dog out of his house to the road side for attending call of nature. He swept the house and went to God's room for lightening evening candles. After evening prayer he came to his drawing room and made a call to Shilpa's cell phone. She replied that they were returning from marriage party and they would reach home by 8P.M. He took his diary and wanted to finish a half completed story. Nothing came to his mind . He went to kitchen ,prepared tea and started sipping a cup of tea. While sipping tea he recollected two incidents that confirmed his conviction on bad luck.

Life very often make us to tom fool. We reject the chances for which we regret later on. It was unforgettable dejavu in life when he refused to accept chance for Govt, service. In those days he and the odia lecturer of his college used to attend college in a scooter. One day he said to Manas;

I am going to give rupees to the minister of tourism for sappointment in the post of Additional District Public Relation Officer. You should join with me. Many posts are vacant. The minister has given assurance to give appointment letter within two years. We have to give our resumes, attested copies of certificates and money. My brother- in- law is very close to the minister. The amount is not high. It is 5000 only.

Manas laughed and said;

I Don't believe in the assurance of that primary school passed drunkard and lewd minister who has got portfolio on SC quota.

The odia lecturer said nothing and the matter ended. After one and half year he got Govt. appointment as ADPRO , Balasore. Manas became very unhappy and regretted for his bad luck.

In the same way he turned down the offer to join in a college where he would have got full GIA of 1994. He got 40% Block Grant after 15 years of working in the college with sundry salary.

Those incidents made him learn from life that sometimes we become fool enough to reject the best chances and to make blunders because of bad luck or good luck that time decides and vindicate all our analysis worthless till the final end of life.

His wife and children arrived at home. He had no time to waste for worthless analysis what was, what is and what would be.

Epilogue

Life is a big university. All ups and downs of life are the prescribed syllabus as to one's lot. The experiences of life are research papers. The outcomes from zest for life despite ups and downs are thesis with remarks for learning how to bypass worthless analysis of the past and the present without arriving at the final decree of life.

Author's Memoir

I have nothing so great or grand to be introduced. Born in a remote village and having completed all my academic education within my native state, I have led a simple middle-class life. My family and the people of my village are immense sources of joy in my heart.

I prefer to spend more time in the serene countryside, among the innocent villagers who gather in tea shops and betel shops to hold informal assemblies. They discuss various topics, from the progress of our state to the incredibility of India, and even international happenings. I find immense delight in listening to their conversations.

As a teacher, I experience genuine contentment when I have a book to immerse myself in, pouring out my emotions. This activity brings me real pleasure and quenches my thirst for learning. A post-graduate in English literature and now a teacher of English in a junior college in Odisha, I have cultivated a deep love for English literature and language. It offers me a free and spontaneous medium for expressing the emotions, feelings, and consciousness stored within my heart.

The English language, to me, feels like a scientific, concise, and logical chariot—an ideal vehicle for achieving accuracy and precision. Beyond this, the vastness of Jagannath culture and the profound philosophical, religious, and artistic treasures of Odia heritage embody the essence of both Eastern and Western thoughts. These treasures, particularly the idea of self-sacrifice for the salvation of mankind, inspire and enrich my perspectives.

www.ingramcontent.com/pod-product-compliance
Lightning Source LLC
La Vergne TN
LVHW041107150826
845673LV00007B/1962